Annie AND THE MOVIE STAR

A Lake Sterling Romance

AMY SPARLING

Copyright © 2022 by Amy Sparling

All rights reserved.

No part of this book may be reproduced in any form or by any electronic or mechanical means, including information storage and retrieval systems, without written permission from the author, except for the use of brief quotations in a book review.

CHAPTER 1

Annie

This has been a terrible day. One day your boss is giving you a coffee mug with a gift card that says you're a hero for being a nurse, and the next day, that very same boss frowns at you with this fake sadness in his voice as he informs you that you no longer have a job. That they're closing down the urgent care center you work for, and that your contract has been cancelled, you don't get severance pay, and *good luck finding a new job!*

Tears float in the corners of my eyes. I've never cried in public and I don't intend to, but a few minutes later I lose the battle of keeping them at bay. I'm fully crying now as I walk to my car, my lunch kit dangling from my wrist and a box of my possessions in my hands. It's not much—just photos and trinkets that sat on my part of the nurse desk. One purple computer mouse I'd brought from home. And a little trophy my best friend Julie gave me that says World's Best Nurse.

I'm the world's nothing now because I'm jobless. Unemployed. Not exactly fired, but *let go*.

More tears fall down my cheeks as I pack my stuff into the backseat of my car and then climb inside. I know it isn't the worst thing in the world, but it sucks. I loved my job. I loved working the night shift, and I especially loved the pay. It's what enabled me to pay off my student loans in record time, then pay off my parents' mortgage so they wouldn't have to struggle anymore. I don't even have any family here in Dallas, Texas. They're all up in New Jersey. I was just living here in my too-small garage apartment because the pay was so good. Yet now here I am with no job and no savings because I only just now finished paying off my parents' house for them. It was my life's goal, and I'm glad I did it. My parents worked so hard over the years and they gave me everything they could. Paying off their mortgage so they can retire early is the most important thing I've ever done. But over the past few years, I wasn't contributing to my savings because I stupidly thought this job would last forever.

I gave everything to my job. I even put off dating, choosing to work the night shift that no one else likes because it pays more, even though it means I have no social life. But in the end, it didn't matter that I gave everything to my job. You can love your job, but your job will never love you back.

I sulk the entire drive back home. I decide to spend the evening eating ice cream and watching TV and allowing myself to be sad, then first thing tomorrow morning I'll look for a new job. This heartbreaking change was so unexpected and I deserve to sulk a little bit. But then I'll wake up early tomorrow and start filling out job applications.

Only when I get home to my adorable, yet small garage apartment, I find my landlords standing next to a moving truck that's blocking my parking spot.

Mr. and Mrs. Newman are an older couple who live in the house on the property. Their garage apartment is a separate building set off to the side of the main house, and they've rented it to me for two years. I don't see them very often since I work the night shift, but I do come home around eight in the morning so sometimes I'll see Mr. Newman drinking coffee on his porch and we'll share some friendly small talk. I see Mrs. Newman on the weekends sometimes while we're both leaving to run errands. They're nice people.

I wipe the tears from my eyes and try to look like I haven't been crying as I get out of my car. "Good morning," I say, sounding like a cheerful happy woman who didn't just lose her job. "Who's moving?"

"You are, I'm afraid," Mr. Newman says.

Confusion makes me laugh at first. Then the look on their faces tells me that something is terribly wrong because they aren't laughing. They're staring at me like I'm an inconvenience, not a friend.

"I'm moving?" I ask. I don't recall deciding to move.

Mrs. Newman gives me a sad little smile and she walks over to me, putting a hand on my arm. "I'm sorry honey, but we decided to let our son move back in because he's fallen on some hard times and he needs a place to stay."

I'm all for helping out people who have fallen on hard times, but their son is a piece of work. He's always coming over just to borrow money from them, and they always complain about it to me. They should stand up to him and stop giving him everything he wants. He's like forty years old. Plus, we all know he's not going to pay them rent to stay in the garage apartment. I do.

"He can't just move into your house?" I ask. It's a pretty big house. I'm sure it has way more than one bedroom in it. It's two stories tall and massive!

"He's a grown man," Mrs. Newman says. "He deserves his own place and some privacy."

Her husband nods and says, "Plus, your lease has been up for over a year now. You've technically been renting from us on a month-to-month basis now, so it's within our right to ask you to leave and not renew you for another month."

I swallow. I guess that's true. But a little advance notice would have been nice.

He continues, "You have three days to move out, but if you can do it faster that would be good because my son has to keep renting this moving truck each day it sits here."

Here's the thing. I'm a nice person. I'm friendly and kind, and I go out of my way to help people. But I just lost my job and my apartment in the same day. With zero advanced notice on either one of them. I have maybe four hundred dollars in the bank. I can't believe this is happening. But it is happening. And it's crappy and unfair if you ask me. And even though I'm a nice person, the fact that my landlords moved their son's stuff over here before even officially telling me I have to move out makes me angry in a way I can't explain, and that's why what I say next isn't very nice at all.

"You're both bad people," I say, putting as much

venom in my voice as I can. I'm never mean, so it's not like I have practice. In fact, I deal with grumpy patients all the time and I never, ever, raise my voice with them. But this is different. I grit my teeth, taking satisfaction in the insulted expression on both of their faces. "Don't worry, though. You're bad people but I'm a good person, so I'll be out of here tomorrow so you can have plenty of time to move in your pathetic, deadbeat son."

One SUV of stuff.

That's my life. My whole life.

The garage apartment came fully furnished when I first rented it, so everything I own can be loaded into my SUV, minus some trinkets and stuff that I loaded up this morning and dropped off at a thrift store. It only took a few hours to pack up, which I did last night because I was so angry and upset that I wasn't able to sleep much. I start my car and drive away from the place that had been my quiet, clean home for two years. I go straight to a gas station and fill up my tank, and then I sit in the parking lot for a while, wondering what on earth I'm going to do.

I just want to scream but screaming won't solve anything.

I don't want my parents to worry about me, plus they're not even in the country right now. They're in the Philippines spending time with my cousins, which they were able to afford this month because they no longer have a mortgage payment. If I were to call them and tell them what happened, they'd only worry and then tell me to move in with them, but they own a very small condo that's filled with my dad's baseball memorabilia and my mom's quilting supplies. There's not even enough room for me to sleep on the couch at their place. I love my parents, but I'd go crazy being stuck in their condo. I need to handle this on my own.

So I call my best friend.

"Hey Annie!" Julie says when she answers my video chat call. "What's up?"

My best friend's brown hair is pulled into a messy bun—her classic writer hair style—and she's sipping coffee while on her back patio. Her patio isn't a usual patio. It faces Lake Sterling, and it's huge, nearly the size of the entire house. She has beautiful patio furniture, so it's like an outdoor living room. It's where she likes to get some writing done, outside facing the lake, the sun warming her skin.

"I'm sorry to bother you but..." I stop, swallow,

and then get the courage to say it. I don't want to be a burden, but I don't have much choice right now. "Can I come stay with you for a few days?"

"Of course," she says, setting her coffee mug down. "How did you find the time off work to come visit?"

"I was laid off."

Her eyes widen on my phone screen. "Oh Annie! I'm so sorry!"

And I lost my apartment, I think. But I can't bring myself to tell her that second bit of bad news right now. I don't want to put all my problems onto my best friend. I just need a few days with her so I won't rack up a ton of debt paying for hotel rooms, and also so I have a friendly face to cheer me up. Then I'll find a new job, and I'll get a new apartment. I just need a few days.

We talk a bit longer, mostly about how her new novel is coming along. When our call is over, I set my GPS for her adorable lakefront house in a super tiny Texas town called Sterling that's about six hours away from Dallas, and I set off on my adventure. Okay, maybe it's not an *adventure*. It's not a new job and it's not an official place to live, but at least I have something to do. It sure beats sitting here in this gas station parking lot.

Once I'm only about forty-five minutes away

from Sterling, I have to pee. I wish I could push on and wait until I'm at Julie's house, but when nature calls, you must answer. I exit the interstate and find a gas station that has a diner next to it. Since gas station bathrooms are extremely yuck, I walk over to the diner, needing to pee more urgently with each passing second.

This little diner has only one unisex bathroom. And it's currently locked. I can see the light on underneath the door, so I step back and wait. And wait. And wait.

Maybe you need a key or something to get inside this bathroom? Walking back to the counter, I ask but the waitress tells me there's no key, so someone must be using the bathroom.

I walk back and tap lightly on the door. "Hello?"

"Uh, just a minute," a male voice says from the other side.

Then it sounds like a hair dryer turns on. I lift an eyebrow. All kinds of sounds come from the bathroom, but not normal sounds. No toilet flushing sounds like what you would expect. The sink turns on once. Then I hear some clanking and moving. Then the sound of a long zipper, like maybe the zipper on luggage?

What on earth is going on in there?

I knock again. "Other people need to use this restroom," I call out.

"Just a minute!" the voice says again.

I grit my teeth and try not to do a classic *I have to pee dance* right here in the back of a small diner.

I knock again.

"Almost done."

The zipper sound happens again. I am seriously considering abandoning all hope and running to the gross gas station bathroom next door, but then the door opens. A stupidly gorgeous man steps out, wearing jeans and a T-shirt with a blue and black button-up flannel shirt on top, the buttons undone. He wears a blue beanie on his head, but dark hair pokes out the bottom.

He's also wearing sunglasses, even though he's indoors. The way he turns to look at me, and that stupid grin he gives me tells me he probably doesn't have a vision disability. So he's one of those people— people who wear sunglasses inside because they think it makes them look cool. News flash: it does not.

My eyesight must be playing tricks on me, however, because he's the most gorgeous man I've ever seen. And surely, the most gorgeous man I've ever seen wouldn't be this much of a selfish jerk.

"Finally," I snap, refusing to let my expression

reveal that I think he's hot.

"I wasn't in there very long," he says, looking away. He reaches back into the bathroom and carries out two suitcases. That explains the zipper noises, I guess.

"This is a bathroom, not a changing room, you know. You're not special. You're supposed to pee and get out, just like everyone else."

"Sorry you had to wait," he says, not looking at me. In fact, it's almost like he's deliberately not looking at me by focusing on the floor instead. Why? Does he think he's better than me? Does he think that his suitcases and stupid sunglasses are more important than having basic human courtesy and letting other people use the restroom? *Ugh.*

"The world doesn't revolve around you," I snap, stepping out of his way so he can haul his dumb suitcases down the small hallway.

"I'm sorry," he says, holding up his hands in surrender. "It's all yours now."

He still isn't looking at me, and I don't know why. Plus I don't have time to analyze it. All I know is that he's rude. And I hate him.

And he's super hot, but whatever. It's not like his hotness matters.

"I would love to keep telling you how rude you're being," I say to his back. "But I have to pee!"

CHAPTER 2

Trevor

After being (rightfully) confronted by someone for hogging the bathroom too long, I quickly rush out of the diner and back to my car, a nondescript blue sedan that I got at the car rental place. In LA, I'll happily cruise around in my sports car—a brand new shiny black Camaro that I paid cash for after my first feature film—but here in the middle-of-nowhere, I learned very quickly that I need to blend in with average people so I'm not recognized.

Living and acting in Los Angeles for the last two years has made me forget what it's like to be out and about in the rest of the country. Or maybe things are just different now. I've acted in a few TV shows and have had three feature films to my name now, and people are starting to recognize me. Entertainment magazines have dubbed me America's Sweetheart, for being a nice guy who plays the romantic lead in wholesome family-friendly movies. I have a reputation now, and just a few years ago, I was a nobody. It's still weird to me because I feel like the same guy I've always been. But then I go out in public and I'm swarmed by fans who want to touch me and grab me and take pictures with me. It's not that I'm not grateful for the fans, but sometimes I just want to be treated like a regular guy.

I'm about to start filming my fourth film with the same production company—yet another wholesome romance called *Oakbrook Lake*. The film crew chose a small Texas town for filming, and I'm due to arrive at the hotel today. I chose to drive to Texas rather than fly because I thought I'd be fun. I was getting tired of living the actor's life in LA and I wanted some time alone to myself on the wide open road, and a road trip sounded like a lot of fun. The only downside to the road trip is that wide open roads for thirteen hundred miles means you have to make lots of pit stops for fuel and food.

Lots of pit stops mean encountering lots of people. Many of those people recognize me as Trevor Owens, America's Sweetheart movie star. After one stop for lunch, I had two women follow me in their car, honking their horn and trying to get my attention near the New Mexico border. I had to exit somewhere random and drive around for half an hour before I finally lost them. Every other stop I've made has been a nightmare of women recognizing me and throwing themselves at me. When I was thirteen, I would have loved all the attention.

But now at 29, I can't stand it.

It's one thing to meet fans during a press event, but I don't like being hounded when I'm just trying to stop somewhere for a quick meal. This whole road trip has been stressful, not relaxing like I'd wanted it to be. I should have just taken a plane, flown first class, and arrived with only minimal "famous people" problems in the airport. Sometimes I seriously question why I'm doing this career in the first place.

Then I remember my mom. The absolute saint of a woman who is battling breast cancer after losing everything and going broke when my dad died and they were drowning in debt but she didn't know it. Mom didn't have any insurance when she was diagnosed a few years ago, and her medical bills bankrupted her even more than the debt had. I'd been fresh out of college, working an entry-level job that didn't pay very much when it all went down. I quickly left my apartment and moved in with my mom to help her out with the bills, but it wasn't enough.

That's when I signed up for a casting call I heard about on the radio. I loved acting in plays throughout junior high and high school, but had never considered it as a career before. But the radio ad had captured my attention in a surreal way. I couldn't stop thinking about it, so I went and I auditioned. Soon after, I was cast as Terry the Trainer on a sitcom television show and my acting career got started. Then I was picked up to act in wholesome romance movies, and I moved to LA to do this gig full time, and quickly became America's Sweetheart.

I do this job for my mom. Sure, the fame can be fun. But it's also exhausting. Even with the parts that annoy me, it doesn't matter because at the end of the day, my mom's bills are covered, her debt is paid, her cancer is in remission, and she doesn't have to lift a finger or worry about anything. After raising me and my brothers all our lives, she deserves this.

Yesterday, I arrived in Texas a day earlier than scheduled because all the touristy things I had wanted to do on my drive over here didn't work out. People recognized me everywhere I went, so now I'm under cover. And since I'll be staying in Sterling, Texas for an entire day before my team gets here, I need to be as unrecognizable as possible.

Hence the disguise.

I pulled over at a diner and changed my clothes, sprayed my hair with temporary hair color I got at a pharmacy store, and put on a beanie I found on the same store's clearance rack. The beanie was perfect because I'm Trevor Owens, and Trevor Owens does not wear beanies. Plus he has light brown hair, not black. Add the sunglasses and the extremely tight jeans —also something I don't wear—and I look like a different person.

I hope.

I also shaved my scruffy beard shiny smooth. I'm known for my scruffy beard, and losing the hair changes my appearance. I didn't mean to take up all that time in the bathroom, but I had no other choice. Plus, I had no idea there was only one bathroom in the entire diner, or I would have chosen somewhere else to make my transformation.

So yeah, I feel bad for monopolizing the bathroom that other people needed to use, but I had no choice. And the old me—the non-famous me—would have apologized profusely for upsetting that woman. The old me would have also noticed how stunningly gorgeous she was and asked her on a date right then and there. I wouldn't have been able to wait for a weekend evening to have dinner—I'd ask her to have lunch with me right then and there. I'd have sent prayers up to heaven asking for her to be single so I'd have a chance.

Because that woman, whoever she is, was beautiful. She had long black hair and a heart-shaped face with dark, captivating eyes.

I hate that I avoided her when she confronted me, but I didn't want her to recognize who I am. While I think my disguise is pretty good, who knows if it'll actually fool anyone. What if she had noticed that I'm Trevor Owens and then turned into one of my crazed fans?

I'm way too close to Sterling, Texas for comfort. She could have told everyone that I'm here and then it'd be even harder to stay anonymous.

So while I wish I could have stayed, apologized, and asked her on a date, I had to be cold and distant and rude on purpose, even though I hated every second of it.

It sucks, too, because now I'm back in my boring rental car and daydreaming up alternate realities where I'm not famous and could have asked her on a date.

I wonder if she would have said yes.

CHAPTER 3

Annie

I still can't get over how cute Julie's lake house is. It's a white house with dark blue shutters and a big wraparound porch. It's small, but it's adorable, and it's perfect for just one person. Or for her and Max when he finally proposes. He's already asked me for her ring size so I know the proposal is coming soon. I can't wait. Julie may have gotten famous for her *Love Sucks* novel series about a private investigator who hates love, but Julie herself loves love. She's my best friend and the most worthy person of finding her true soul mate and living out her life in marital bliss.

I'm super excited for the new life she's found here in Sterling after she left her crap-tastic ex. Now I just have to find a way to get my own life back on track. I'm sitting here in my car, parked in her driveway for all of two seconds before the front door opens and my best friend comes rushing out, a big smile on her face.

"Annie!" Julie gushes, throwing me in a hug the moment I exit my car. "I'm so glad you're here. I've missed you so much."

"Me too," I say, squeezing her back. It feels great to hug my best friend. "I'm glad to be here. I just wish it were under better circumstances."

"You'll find a new job soon," she assures me. "You're the world's greatest nurse, after all. Every hospital in the world will want you."

"I'd actually love to work at a retirement home," I say, because that's always been my real goal. As a kid, my grandma lived at an elderly living facility and the nurses were so nice and patient and caring. They inspired me to become a nurse myself.

"Well then you will be the world's greatest retirement home nurse," Julie says.

I chuckle at her optimism, but her words do make me feel a little better, even if everything feels so hopeless lately. She glances toward my car's back door. "Let me get your bag for you."

"No!" I say, stepping in between her and my car. If she opens that door, she'll see that my car has been jam-packed with all my belongings. Then she'll know what happened. I can't let her know that I'm homeless… not yet. I know she's my best friend and she won't judge me, but it feels like admitting my situation to her will be accepting my situation. And I can't accept it just yet. I need to take a few days to see if I can find a job and fix my life before everything falls apart.

"You're my guest," Julie says with a smile. "Let me help you."

"It's no big deal," I say, forcing my voice to sound nonchalant. "I'm actually starving. Do you think we could get some food at that diner you're always raving about?"

Her eyes sparkle at the mention of food, which is something we both love, probably more than we should. "Sounds good," she says. "I'll drive us since you just spent so much time on the road."

I breathe a sigh of relief. Julie didn't see inside my car. And luckily the windows are tinted pretty dark. My secret is safe for now.

Roger's Diner is just a quick drive down the road. It's famous for the delicious food and the view since it has a large patio that overlooks Lake Sterling. Julie talked about the food nonstop when she first moved here. It's also her favorite date night place to go with Max, even though there are nicer restaurants on the lake. This place is just special to them.

Julie leads me to her favorite table on the patio and

then we're greeted by the most cheerful waitress I've ever met. With a big mess of white-blonde hair and bright red lipstick, she's sure to brighten anyone's day. Even someone who just lost their job and apartment. She introduces herself as Clare, then she beams at me.

"Is this the famous Best Friend Annie I've heard so much about?"

"Yep," Julie says, gesturing toward me as if I'm a prize on a game show. "She's visiting me for a few days, so expect to see us here three times a day."

"I'll keep your favorite table free for you," Clare says with a wink. Then she takes our order. Julie is so excited to show me her favorite diner that she orders fried pickles, cheese sticks, and the queso for appetizers, promising me that I'll love all of them. After a quick look at the menu, I order a good old-fashioned cheeseburger, waffle fries, and a vanilla milkshake since I'm still pretty sad about my life situation, despite being with my best friend. Drowning my sorrow in food and sugar sounds pretty good right about now.

"So how's the boyfriend?" I ask, giving her a silly wiggle of my eyebrows as I snack on fried pickles. (She was right, the pickles with the diner's homemade ranch dressing are incredible.)

"Perfect," she says, grinning back at me. "I hate

that he's out of town for a job this week but it kind of works out perfectly since you're here now."

"Where's he working?" I ask, reaching for another pickle.

"He's over in Apple Valley doing a quick flip for his friend. The guy thought he could buy a house, fix it up, and make a huge profit selling it again but he's a terrible handyman. So he hired Max to do the work and they're going to split the profits when the house sells. Max has been really into doing big jobs that pay a lot lately."

"I wonder why..." I say in a singsong voice.

She doesn't seem to catch on that I'm insinuating the likelihood of a marriage proposal, because her brows crunch together in confusion. She takes a bite of a fried mozzarella stick. "Huh?"

"He's earning big money so he can *save big money*," I say, making air quotes. "It must be for *something special*."

"Like what? A new car or something?"

Oh my gosh, I love Julie, but she is so clueless right now!

I roll my eyes. "I'm just...*proposing* the idea that maybe Max is considering a *proposal* of his own..."

Her eyes widen as she finally gets what I've been hinting at. Then her cheeks turn pink. "Oh my gosh!

No way... I mean, yeah I think we both want to get married one day but it's too soon. He's probably not even thinking about that right now."

I'm in one of those ethical sticky situations at the moment because I know for a fact that her boyfriend is absolutely thinking about proposing. Since she's my best friend, I kind of have a moral obligation to tell her. But her boyfriend also came to me in confidence when he was trying to figure out her ring size without her knowing. I promised him I wouldn't tell her that he'd reached out to me so as to keep it all a surprise, so I also owe him that. It's my best friend duty to take care of Julie, but in this case, I think it's better if I keep my mouth shut. Her surprise when he proposes will totally be worth it. I'm sure she'll forgive me.

I shrug and reach for another fried pickle. "I'm just playing with you. But at least you've got a man who likes to earn money. He's got ambition. He's a total keeper."

"Plus he's extremely gorgeous," she says, gazing up at the sky while she swoons over her own boyfriend. It's adorable. And slightly annoying to those of us who are pathetic single people with no job or apartment.

My heart twinges a little, but I shove the pain aside. I'm not here to sully my best friend's happiness. Luckily, Clare walks out with our entrées which means I can now stuff myself with food instead of sad feelings and fried pickles.

A short while later, a group of four young women come bursting through the back doors of the diner that lead to the patio. They're loudly talking and… I don't know how to describe it other than "fangirling" over something. They look exactly like how Julie and I looked that time we got to meet our favorite boyband after their Houston show. Their faces are filled with excitement and their voices are high-pitched and they keep talking all over each other as they make their way to a table.

"Whoa, who gave them too much coffee?" Julie asks.

I snort. "Reminds me of us."

"No way, we were never that bad," she says with a chuckle.

I click my tongue. "Yes we were! We can fangirl like no other. Remember that boyband when we were in high school? Or when we went to all those midnight movie premiers as teenagers?"

"Hey, no one can blame us for obsessing over Twilight," she says, pointing a finger at me.

We keep eating our lunch while trying to over-hear whatever it is that has those women so excited. They keep looking at their phones then showing the screen to each other. It looks like they're on the Twitter app, but I can't be sure. I admit, I'm curious, but not trying to be a creepy eavesdropper at the same time.

When Clare brings us drink refills, Julie leans in and whispers, "What are they talking about?"

Clare glances over at their table then looks back at us, eyes wide with enthusiasm. "You haven't heard? About the movie?"

Julie cocks an eyebrow. "What movie?"

"Some Hollywood movie company is filming a romance movie right here in Sterling! Apparently it's been in the works for a while and the town kept it kind of hush hush, but the film crew arrived today, out at the hotel by the water. Some hottie actor is staring in the movie so those girls are trying to figure out a way to meet him."

"Wow," Julie and I say at the exact same time.

"Who's the actor?" I ask.

Clare shrugs. "I'm too old for that stuff, darlin'. I never know who these famous young celebrities are, but I know it's not George Clooney or I'd be down there breaking onto the set myself. Now he is one fine piece of man." She chuckles at her own joke as she walks away.

Julie does a little Google research on her phone.

"It's Trevor Owens," she says, reading from the screen.

"Trevor Owens?" The name sounds familiar but I'm not good with celebrity names.

"And the female lead is Andrea Block," Julie says.

That name I do recognize. "Wow, she's really famous."

Julie nods while scrolling through her phone. "The movie is called *Oakbrook Lake*, and it's one of those cheesy romance movies with a totally obvious plot."

"So, like, our favorite thing to watch?"

She grins. "Yep. It sounds cute. This is exciting. And the guy is pretty hot."

She turns her phone to me, showing me a picture of Trevor Owens. I may not be good at remembering celebrity names, but this guy looks familiar. I think I've seen some of his films, if they're the kind I'm thinking of. Maybe he was in one of the Christmas romances I watched last year...I can't quite put my finger on it, but I know I've seen him before.

Then the hair on the back of my neck prickles. My jaw drops. This guy on Julie's phone screen has a scruffy beard and lighter hair... but I can't help but think that he looks an awful lot like that rude guy in the gas station.

Did I meet a celebrity and not realize it?

CHAPTER 4

Trevor

It's four in the morning and I actually feel refreshed and I'm ready to take on the work of filming a new movie. Usually waking up for an early call time is miserable, but I got a great night's sleep at the Lake Sterling Hotel. Our producer booked the entire hotel for the duration of filming, which will only take about two months. There is private security, the parking lot is shut down, and we're safe from the public, which means I slept like a baby after my long, miserable road trip of being recognized a dozen times before I donned my disguise.

I grab some coffee from the hotel lobby and get in the shuttle van with a few other actors and crew members and ride to the set. The two actors who play my parents are here in the shuttle van, and I haven't officially met them yet, so I introduce myself. Even with a few movies and some TV show appearances under my belt, I still feel so new to the world of acting. The woman playing my mom has been on TV shows for decades, and so have many of the cast members, which makes me feel so out of place.

Oakbrook Lake is a sweet romance movie, the kind of feel-good mushy-gushy movies that my own mom loves. That's actually why I auditioned for the first one I was casted in, because I knew my mom would love it. Truth be told, I'm not exactly a "romance movie" fan myself—I prefer action movies—but starring in them has been a good career move. It earned me the title of America's Sweetheart, among other wholesome nicknames. I love that I can act out a part and not have to strip naked or belittle myself. I can keep my values and ethics and create movies that I'm not ashamed of.

Oakbrook Lake will be a little different than the other movies I've starred in. This time I'm staring alongside the famous Andrea Block, an actress who is several times more famous than I am, and working with her will do wonders for my career. Ever since the casting was announced a few months ago, my social media followers skyrocketed. All of this results in more gigs and more money to take care of my mom. Ultimately, that's why I'm here doing this, and I'm extremely grateful for the opportunity.

Once we arrive on set, I'm directed to my trailer which is right next to Andrea Block's trailer. I've actually never met her before. Her assistant is rushing around talking on the phone, all in a tizzy because Andrea hasn't arrived yet. I'd get chewed out by my agent if I were late to a call time, but something tells me the famous Andrea Block will get a break for being a little bit late. She's the highest billed actor for the entire film.

In my trailer, I get another coffee and sit in front of a lighted mirror for hair and makeup. I try making friendly small talk with the guy who does my hair and the woman doing my makeup, but they're all business and don't seem to care for conversation. About an hour later, I'm all set and wearing my outfit for the first scene of filming. Today's scene takes place in a park, which the city has shut down for filming purposes. All the people who will be mulling around in the park are paid extras, not regular citizens.

"Take a seat, Trev," the director, Paul, says. No one calls me "Trev" instead of Trevor, and it's a little weird that he's doing it now. The lines across his forehead are deeper than usual and he looks annoyed. "We're still waiting on Andrea."

"She's still not here?" I ask, looking around.

"She's in hair and makeup," he gruffs before walking away to give directions to some crew member.

When the famous actress finally emerges from her trailer, she's in pajamas with expertly-styled messy hair —the costume she wears for the opening meet-cute scene.

"Hi, Andrea, it's nice to meet you," I say, reaching out my hand to shake.

She looks me up and down, her expression blank. "I have a boyfriend, just so you know," she says, pursing her lips as she stares at me. She doesn't even make an effort to shake my hand, but she does point a finger at me as if I'm a little kid. "So there will be no small talk, and no extra kissing. Keep your hands off me unless we're specifically shooting a scene."

"Okay..." I have no desire to date or flirt with this woman and it's extremely presumptuous of her to think as much. I was just saying hello to the person who will be in nearly every scene with me for the next sixty days. "Can I ask what *extra kissing* means? I'm pretty sure we have to kiss in the script."

In fact, I know we have to kiss in the script because I've read the script but I'm trying to be nice here. I have to kiss someone in every one of these wholesome romance movies I've starred in. It's a romance, after all. That's the point of the entire plot.

"Twice," she snaps, looking at me like I'm the world's biggest idiot. "There are two kiss scenes. I will record each scene in one take, and nothing more. Get it right the first time, or they can just CGI a kiss into the final footage, I don't care. But I'm not here to make friends, TV boy."

TV boy? She said the words like they were an insult, but it's kind of funny and I have to hold back laughter as she turns on her heel and marches over to her starting position near water fountain.

Paul claps me on the back and says, "You'll get used to it. She hates everyone and everyone hates her."

"So why is she in this film?" I ask soft enough for only him to hear.

He chuckles then slides his thumb over his fingers in that gesture that means money. "The studio puts up with a lot for the amount of cash she rakes in. Lucky for you, your fame will grow since you're in the film with her. We all win."

"Riiiight..." I put on a polite smile despite what I'm feeling inside, because I'm a nice guy and Andrea's attitude problem is her problem, not mine. But if it were up to me, I wouldn't hire anyone who walks around treating everyone like crap and pretending the world revolves around them.

We start filming and Andrea becomes a totally different person. She's actually an incredible actress because she transforms from a rude actress to sweet fictional character the moment the director yells, "Action!"

Andrea's playing the love interest in the film, so she acts like she likes my character, just as the script reads. And then each time the director cuts a scene, she instantly morphs back into a cold, uncaring brat.

It's kind of fascinating. I'm awed at her talent, even if I'm repulsed by her personality.

The first day of filming is long and exhausting, but soon we're on the final scene of the day, which takes place at a banquet hall that overlooks the lake. I'm talking with one of the actors while Andrea does a solo scene, when suddenly a loud shriek fills the air. People rush over to Andrea, who is screaming profanities and crying at the same time.

"What's going on?" I ask our director as he walks by.

"Andrea's arm is broken," he says with anger and disappointment in his voice. "It looks bad. An ambulance is on the way."

"Whoa," I say. "That's awful."

He snorts in agreement. I get the feeling that Andrea Block was casted for this film against his wishes and now he's about to call someone and tell them *I told you so*. But to me, he simply shrugs and says, "You know what they say... the show must go on."

CHAPTER 5

Annie

The panic sets in around midnight. It was easy to hang out with my best friend today, ignoring the truth of my situation, shoving it into the far recesses of my mind while I had fun with Julie in Sterling, Texas. But now I'm all alone on a futon in Julie's office-slash-spare bedroom and the reality of my situation comes crashing down on me.

I need a job.

I don't have much money saved, and even if I start applying for jobs tomorrow morning, it'll take days to get an interview, and a second interview, and a hiring date... and then weeks after that for a paycheck. I need to eat. Julie bought my dinner tonight, but I can't just keep mooching off my best friend. I need a job now.

My dream job is working at a retirement home as

the resident nurse, but right now I'm desperate and I'll take any job. With any luck, maybe I can find a nursing job here in Texas, and I can get an apartment nearby and be close to Julie. I remember how hard it was for her to secure this lake house once she had chosen to move to this adorable small town, so my hopes aren't very high. The real estate isn't exactly booming around here because it's such a small town, and there aren't many homes that don't already have a family living in them. Sterling is the exact opposite of Dallas, where builders are turning every empty piece of land into an apartment complex or neighborhood.

If Sterling is out of the picture, maybe I can find a job and place to live in a nearby city so I'm at least close enough to visit my best friend more often that I've been able to in the last few years. That's really my only criteria—it's not like I'm looking for love any time soon. Men just let me down. I guess I'm lucky that I haven't been horribly cheated on like Julie was in the past, but the men in my life have all been duds. They either care too much about their guy friends, or their jobs, or their gaming addiction to care about me. I'm tired of bouncing around from one boring man who doesn't care about me to the next, which is why I dedicated myself to my job ages ago. All I need in life is a good job and a great place to live that's close to my best friend. I do not need a man.

Whatever I do, I need to do it quickly. I refuse to stay here imposing on Julie for too long. As the night goes on, I toss and turn on the futon and barely get any sleep. Once it's six in the morning, I go ahead and get up, having resigned myself to the idea of getting any sleep tonight. I grab my laptop and quietly walk out Julie's back door to the back patio table to start my job search.

Unfortunately, I lost my last resume years ago, so my first task is writing up a new one, then I apply to a dozen jobs that are within an hour away from Sterling. Then, because I'm worried that's not enough, I apply to even more nursing jobs that are farther way.

A couple hours later, the back patio door opens and Julie, wearing flannel pajama pants and a black tank top, walks out with two cups of coffee.

"Good morning," she says, handing me a cup of coffee. "You're up early."

"I need a job," I say, gratefully taking a big sip of caffeine. "I'm worried I won't find one fast enough and I can't afford to wait much longer."

She sits next to me, glancing at my computer screen. "Why are you searching for jobs around here?"

"Because I'm tired of Dallas."

Her eyes light up. "Wait, are you going to move here? That would be so cool! When is your apartment lease up?"

I bite my lip, not wanting to tell her the truth, but it's kind of too late now. "It's already up. I kind of got kicked out."

"What?" she says, her jaw dropping.

I tell her the story, almost breaking into tears as I recite the callous way my former landlords kicked me out. "And that's why I'm here. It's not a fun visit for me... it's because I'm homeless."

"Oh my gosh," she says, throwing her arms around me. "Annie, I'm so sorry. You can stay here as long as you want."

I shake my head. "I knew you would say that, but no. I'm not going to do that. I need to get out as soon as possible and take care of myself because I'm not going to become a burden on you. I refuse."

"You would never be a burden," she says. "You're my best friend and I'm happy to have you here."

Maybe if we were both single ladies it would be fun to live together as roomies for a while. But that's not the case. Max is on the verge of proposing to Julie. I'm not going to be the bum living in her house, inhibiting all her romantic wedding planning time with Max. I don't want to be the annoying third wheel. Plus, I'm an adult. I need to be on my own.

My laptop chimes.

"Oh yay!" I say as I do a little shimmy dance. "That's the job alert I set up! It means a new nursing job has been posted. Maybe I'll get lucky and it'll be a retirement home job!"

I click the link and my shoulders fall. "Dang, it's just regular nursing, but it's here in Sterling, so that's good."

Julie claps her hands together excitedly. "How cool would it be if you worked here? We'd finally get to hang out every day."

My smile falters as I read the short listing. "It's a contract position that only lasts two months, but I'm going to apply anyway. I could work that job temporarily to have money while I look for a full-time job."

I fill out the short application, attach my resume, and hit send. Julie and I head to Roger's Diner for breakfast, and while the healthy-minded nurse in me cringes at the amount of unhealthy food I scarf down, the other part of me is in foodie heaven. The diner's biscuits and gravy are to die for, and the bacon is extra crispy—my favorite.

Not even an hour after my job application for the

contract position, I get a phone call from someone named Lucia. She asks if I can start work today.

I enthusiastically tell her yes, nearly choking on my biscuits in the process. After the call ends, I tell Julie the good news.

"Yay!" she says, giving me a high five. "When do you start?"

"In two hours." I grab another piece of bacon. "Hopefully I can find a pair of scrubs out of one of the bags in my car."

While the job description and phone call from Lucia were fairly vague, I soon realize that this isn't some nursing job at a local doctor's office, or school, or someplace where you'd expect to need a nurse. It's a film set. I arrive at the address I was given, which is a large park on the outskirts of town, and I have to talk to a security guard, who checks my ID and calls for Lucia to come retrieve me. This is all so surreal and weird. I was expecting to work at a doctor's office, not a film set.

I guess it makes sense that a film crew would need a nurse on site so I can treat minor wounds if they happen to come up. This is actually kind of cool, I realize while I stand here in my pink Hello Kitty scrubs, waiting for Lucia to come give me permission to enter the set.

What if I get a chance to meet the celebrities? I wonder what those girls back at the diner would say about that. Maybe I'll even get to take a picture with the famous Andrea Block or that handsome guy who's playing the lead role. Those girls from the diner would lose their minds if I told them where I am right now.

Finally, a woman wearing all black and driving a golf cart arrives at the security check-in station.

"Annie?" she asks, getting out of the golf cart.

"Yes, ma'am," I reply.

She looks me over. "Wow, you really dressed the part, didn't you?" She chortles, glancing over at the security guard who is also smirking at me in a way that makes me feel stupid. I'm a nurse. Nurses wear scrubs. What's the problem here?

I look down at myself, doing a double-check that I'm actually wearing my pink Hello Kitty scrubs, because I'm suddenly afraid that maybe I forgot to put on pants or something. But no, I'm wearing my favorite white sneakers, and I'm fully clothed.

"Yes ma'am," I say, biting my lip. "Should I be wearing solid colors or something else?"

She laughs and shakes her head. "Honey, you're

just an extra, you can wear whatever the heck you want."

"An extra? Are there more nurses on site?"

"Come on, let's get you on the set," she says, motioning for me to hop on the golf cart with her. She doesn't seem to hear the question I asked, or maybe she's just too busy to care.

I take in the sights of being on a film set—several white trailers, lots of security, box vans, tents, and equipment everywhere. I even see that camera equipment that looks like train tracks and mini cranes that hold up the cameras for different angles.

"I'm sorry," I say, feeling stupid but knowing I need to clarify what the heck she meant. "What do you mean about being an extra? Are there other nurses and I'm the one on standby or something?"

Lucia frowns. "Honey, you're just an extra."

Anxiety rises up my throat. "I'm sorry, I think I got mixed up with someone else. I'm Annie Reyes. I was hired for the nursing position."

She quirks an eyebrow. "Honey, there is no nursing position. What are you talking about?"

I take out my phone and show her the job listing that I applied to. Her brows crinkle together as she reads it.

"Oh my gosh," Lucia says, lowering her head and closing her eyes for a moment. "That intern is the biggest idiot..." She looks up and breathes a deep sigh. "Well, my dear, you are correct. You did apply to a nursing position. But that's not the job we're offering you at all... and I can't believe the intern I tasked with posting a job position would make such a huge mistake."

My pulse quickens as I realize this isn't a nursing job after all. She's going to send me home and I'll be back to where I started with no income and no way to pay my bills.

But then Lucia shrugs. "The actual job is to be a stand-in for Andrea Block, who plays the *nurse character* in this movie. We don't need a real nurse, just a stand-in for someone who plays a fictional nurse. The actress broke her arm, but the filming must continue even without her, so we just need a warm body to be there for the other actors to act around, so we can still get some filming done."

"You want me to fill in for Andrea Block?" I say, barely able to comprehend what I've just said. She's a famous actress. I have never acted a day in my life, unless you count being polite around patients who are getting on my last nerve.

"It's super easy," Lucia continues. "You'll just be

an extra. You won't have to do much. The job is yours if you still want it. What do you say?"

Before I can answer, the hottest man I've ever seen in my life walks up to us. Technically it's the second time I've seen him, but he's even hotter now without that ridiculous beanie and ugly sunglasses. It's Trevor Owens himself, looking just like his picture online, wearing jeans and a tight-fitting white t-shirt, a friendly smile on his gorgeous, chiseled face.

"Hello, are you the Andrea stand-in?"

Our eyes meet. I know without a single shred of doubt that this man right here is the jerk from the bathroom the other day.

I can't believe I'll get paid to stand around and look at this gorgeous man all day. This might be the greatest job on the entire planet. Looks like my string of bad luck has crash landed right into a brick wall of the best luck ever. I nod, realizing I hadn't answered his question.

"Yes. Yes I am."

CHAPTER 6

Trevor

Life can be so weird. Incredibly weird.

Almost unbelievably weird.

Because if you'd told me that I would run into a beautiful woman at a random diner bathroom, and then that I'd magically be working with her a few days later, I wouldn't have believed it. But she's here, in the flesh, wearing extremely cute nurse scrubs.

Her long dark hair is pulled into a sleek, low ponytail and her ears are dotted with small diamond earrings. I don't think she's wearing any makeup, and yet she's beautiful. I'm not exactly an expert or anything, but all the actresses on set wear stage makeup, which is layered on thick with bold colors swept across their eyelids and lips. This woman is fresh-faced.

And still the most beautiful woman ever.

But why? Why is she here? How did this happen?

Last night when we'd wrapped up filming, the producers agreed to hire a stand-in lookalike for Andrea Block's role. It's a bit unusual, but so much money has already been spent on this movie and cancelling everything for several weeks until Andrea's arm is healed would waste a lot of money. So instead, they're using an extra to dress like Andrea so we can film every possible scene we need to without her there, then when her arm is healed enough, the real actress will return to film all the scenes still left over. It's a weird solution, but it works.

And now here I am, meeting the lookalike stand-in for the first time.

"I guess I should have realized something was up when I had to send my height, weight, and photo along with my job application," the woman says, frowning in thought.

"What do you mean?" I ask. Behind us, Lucia answers her cell phone and then zooms off on the golf cart, probably going to put out another metaphorical fire.

The woman gestures to her clothing. "I thought I was accepting a job as an actual nurse."

"What?" I say with a chuckle. "Why?"

She sighs and shakes her head. "It's a long story."

It's a story I can't hear any time soon because a crew member appears and directs us to the set, and soon this mysterious and beautiful woman is whisked off to hair and makeup. I talk with the director about his vision for the upcoming scene today. It's one that's sure to drive the audience wild. In the movie, I play the role of the grumpy landscaper who takes care of the park grounds at the lake. My character is actually a secret millionaire who likes the hard work of gardening, a fact that Andrea Block's character is ashamed to find out once she judges me for being too poor and blue collar.

This is the scene where I'm shirtless, raking leaves across from the lake front coffee shop, and Andrea's character is sipping coffee inside, ogling my sexy body.

I'm not being vain and arrogant here. I actually do have a sexy body. I've been training for months, unable to eat many carbs or sugar, while the film crew's personal trainer whips me into a sculpted, mass of perfection. Don't get me wrong, I'm usually in decent shape. I have been ever since I played soccer in high school—but I've never been in *this* good of shape. I have no body fat. I'm ripped all the time like the cover of some men's fitness magazine. It's exhausting. I spend three hours a day in the gym to stay this way. I can't wait until filming is over and I can go back to being a regularly fit guy, instead of an insanely fit masterpiece.

When the mystery woman—which I have to call her in my head because I don't know her name— appears from hair and makeup, they've put her in the same outfit that Andrea should be wearing and they've covered her long dark locks with a near-identical wig that looks like Andrea's. From the back, you can't even tell she's a different person.

I try to catch her attention so I can smile and say hello as she's walked into the fake coffee shop set, but she doesn't notice. She looks a little freaked out, to be honest. I'm betting she's never done any acting work before. But I'll take working with a shy actress over the snobby brat Andrea any day.

I tell myself to let it go, to stop thinking of this woman. She doesn't matter. She's an extra. This set is filled with extras. I have a scene to film, so I take off my shirt, let a crew member spray me down with fake sweat, and I get to work.

Once the scene is done, I'm actually a little exhausted from raking the same leaves over and over again, but it's finally time for a break. I know I shouldn't, but I look around for Andrea's body-double, finally finding her standing awkwardly by some lighting equipment.

"Hey," I say, waving as I walk over. "Have you been to craft services yet? I'm starving."

"What's that?" she asks.

"It's food," I say. "You hungry?"

"I've been sitting on a film set staring at the same empty cup of coffee for four hours while you raked leaves," she says. "I'm starving."

I laugh and motion for her to follow me. "Right this way, uh—what's your name?"

"Annie," she says.

"Nice to meet you, Annie."

She nods once. "And you're Trevor Owens."

"Yes, I am." I run my hand over my head. "It's weird that everyone knows who I am but I don't know who they are."

"Is that why you were dressed like a fashion disaster wearing sunglasses in a small town diner?"

I stop, nearly tripping over myself, then I regain control of my body again. "So... you recognized me?"

"Not right away, but eventually." She glances at me for just a moment before looking away, just a small split-second look. But even in that short time, her gaze makes my stomach burst into butterflies. "My friend was talking about the movie getting filmed here and she showed me a picture of the *fancy movie star guy*," she says, her voice getting sarcastic at the end, "and I suddenly realized the movie star was the same jerk who almost made me pee myself in public."

I wince. "I really am sorry. I didn't realize there was just one bathroom and I was in there trying to disguise myself."

She rolls her eyes. "Well, you didn't do a very good job of it, now did you?"

I grin. She's cute even when she's mad at me.

This is not good. Not good at all. In fact, it's really, really bad.

This whole actor-movie-star gig? It's a sham. It's a big fake personality that I put on while playing fake roles and fake pretending to be someone the fans want you to be while you're on camera or signing auto-graphs at some convention. It's all just one be persona my manager and I concocted together when I got my first role. Was I going to be the womanizer bad boy actor or the charming America's sweetheart?

I chose sexy but nice. And it's not really me. It's just my actor self. I mean, sure, I am a nice guy. Deep down, I'm friendly and trustworthy. But I've been pretending to be America's sweetheart for so long that it's kind of hard to remember who exactly I used to be.

There's a dark side to this industry. Everyone

knows about it and yet people keep flocking to it. Fame hurts people. Fame results in multiple broken marriages, drama plastered all over trashy magazines. Embarrassing candid photos from the paparazzi. I'm trying my best to avoid all of that, to work hard on screen but stay in the shadows off screen because I'm only here to earn enough money to make my mom set for life. And, if I'm being honest, I'd like to be set for life, too.

Once I'm rich enough to have both of us taken care of, I'll leave Hollywood and move out to the middle of nowhere and life my life quietly and peacefully.

And until that happens, I can't let myself develop a crush on some woman I'll never see again once filming wraps. After all, it's the number one rule of acting:

Never fall in love with your co-star.

CHAPTER 7

Annie

I guess I've never really thought about it, but when you watch the credits at the end of a film, there are a ton of people's names listed. There are also a ton of people here on set. People who aren't actors, but the behind-the-scenes folks who keep the show running. Everything is a whirlwind of chaos—or at least it feels that way to me. I get the feeling that all the people going in all directions between scenes actually know what they're doing. The chaos around me is orderly and everyone else understands it except for me.

Trevor and I talked a bit, but when he says he's going to lead me to "craft services", we get so tangled up in other people that the conversation naturally wanes. Eventually, he turns the corner and the crowds of people thin out. He opens his arms at a white temporary tent, the kind with plastic windows on the plastic walls, and says, "Ta-da! Craft services."

I lift an eyebrow.

"It's food," he says with a big grin. This grin more charming than the grin he has in all those Google images I saw with Julie. It's like he means it this time, and those other times were just for the cameras. "Craft services is the best part of being on a film set," he says, walking toward the plastic door flap. "Unless you're one of those women who refuse to eat?"

Briefly, I have a teensy thought that he's making fun of my weight. I'm not a rail-thin woman like most of the actresses he's probably used to working with. I have curves.

But he seems friendly, so maybe he's not insinuating anything at all. Maybe he's just used to actresses who don't want to eat.

I shrug. "Depends on how good the food is."

A young guy wearing black skinny jeans and a black T-shirt holds out his hand to stop us before we walk inside the tent.

"Actors only," he says, looking at me with a polite, yet annoyed expression.

"She's with me," Trevor says.

"She's an extra," the guy says back without missing a beat. Something tells me he doesn't get starstruck over celebrities like most people.

"She's the stand-in for the main character, who isn't here because of an injury, which makes her the main character for today," Trevor says.

The guy's brow furrows a bit but then he nods. "Just until Andrea Block returns, I guess."

"I feel bad," I say softly as Trevor leads me into the tent. "I shouldn't be here. I'm not a real actor."

"You deserve to be here," Trevor says. "You spent hours working just now and you deserve to eat."

I look around at the spread of food and my jaw drops. The whole tent is lined with tables that are filled with food. Bagels, chips, candy, fruit, salads, wraps, veggies, sushi, sandwiches, a huge variety of drinks— the list goes on.

"How do we pay for this?" I ask, glancing around at the room that's filled with food but otherwise empty of people.

"It's all part of being an actor," Trevor says, grabbing a cookie and taking a bite. He hands me a sturdy paper plate. "Dig in."

I put a few things on my plate, still feeling guilty about it after what the guy at the door had said. More actors enter the tent to get food, and soon Trevor is the center of attention. The actors are talking about scenes, Andrea Block, and all kinds of stuff. I feel completely out of place, so I take my plate and slip outside, hoping to find a nice shady tree to sit under and eat.

A crew member sees me and gives me much the same look the last guy had.

"Extras wait over there." He points across the park to an area where a few dozen people are hanging out, some sitting on folding chairs and some sitting on the grass. Others have blankets spread out on the ground, as if they knew they'd be stuck waiting around all day and came prepared.

"Thanks," I mumble as I make my way over there.

A plastic bi-fold sign sits on the grass. EXTRA WAITING AREA, is all it says.

I recognize a few of the people from the café scene I sat through earlier. A young woman about my age, with blond hair and heavy makeup waves at me when she sees me.

"Come sit over here," she says, patting the extra space on her blanket on the ground. "You're Andrea Block's stand-in, right?"

"Yep," I say. "I'm Annie."

"I'm Jackie." Her smile turns to shock when she sees my plate. "You're not supposed to eat at craft services. It's for the real actors only, not us." She pats the lunch kit next to her. "We have to bring our own food."

"Yeah, I discovered that a little too late after Trevor told me to go with him." I suck in air through my teeth at the memory of that guy looking down on me like I'm some kind of peasant. "I won't make that mistake again."

"Wait... *the* Trevor Owens told you to go to craft services?" Her eyes are wide and excited, like she's just heard something extra scandalous.

I shrug. "I guess he thought it would be okay since I was filling in for Andrea Block, but the guy totally griped at me for it, so it was awkward."

"Oh my gosh, you're so lucky you got to talk to him," she says, biting her lip like a schoolgirl with an epic crush. "I keep hoping I'll get the chance, but so far they haven't even used me in a scene yet."

"So you just sit here all day?" I ask.

"Yep. Extras hang out until they're needed. If you're lucky, you'll get selected for a non-speaking role. Like being someone who gets coffee spilled on them or something. Then if you're extremely lucky, they'll have you say a line, which means you can get your SAG membership."

"I have no idea what any of that means," I say with a chuckle as I eat the food I'm technically not supposed to have.

"Girl, how do you not know about SAG?"

"I'm not an actress," I say with a shrug. "I'm a nurse. I thought I was being offered a nursing job but it ended up being a stand-in job for the character playing a nurse."

Jackie cocks an eyebrow like she can't believe the story I'm telling her.

I sigh. "Trust me, it's exactly as weird as it sounds. But I need the money so I'm here until I find a better job."

"Wow," Jackie says. "You're not even trying to get up close and personal with the celebrities, and you got to hang out with Trevor Owens on your first day. You are just filled with luck." She leans over and rubs her elbow against mine. "Hopefully some of your luck will wear off on me," she says with a snort of laughter.

"How long have you been doing this?" I ask as I nibble on some food.

"Two years. I'm working to pay for my college."

"Do you make much money as an extra?" I'm not sure if the money I'm earning for the next two months are standard salary or maybe a bit more since I'm standing in for the main actress, but it's not much money at all.

"Nah," she says, waving her hand. "I'm in it for the side benefits..." She wiggles her eyebrows.

"What does that mean?"

"Trevor Owens is quickly becoming a hot commodity." She holds up her phone, wiggling it as if the very existence of her phone answers my question.

"Are you trying to date him?" I guess.

She barks out a laugh. "Ugh, I wish. I mean, sure. If he wants to, I'd date him in a heartbeat, but I am a realistic, practical woman so I know that'll never happen. What I'm saying is that candid photos of Trevor Owens are going for more and more money as he gets more famous. I talked through email with two guys from the media who are offering twenty-five thousand dollars for a candid shot of Trevor. Even more money if I can catch him doing something that goes against his nice guy persona."

My eyes widen. "You mean like... paparazzi type photos?"

She grins. "Heck yeah. The studio is really big on security so they have the whole set blocked off and no one can get in to sneak photos. But extras can."

"That's allowed?"

She blows a raspberry with her tongue. "Girl, no. Of course not. But you just gotta be sneaky about it, ya know? This morning I pretended to be lost for an hour so I could hang around his trailer and hope to catch him in some provocative position, but he arrived with a bunch of other actors and did absolutely nothing picture-worthy. Ugh."

She puts her phone back on the blanket next to her and taps the screen. "But I've got two months to find something. If Andrea Block comes back to set soon, I'll be keeping an eye on her, too. I could get a cool fifty grand for photos of that stuck up witch doing something she shouldn't."

I can't believe what I'm hearing. It's bad enough that actors have paparazzi following them around when they go out to eat and stuff, but on their own film set? Seems awfully intrusive.

"Since you're standing in for the main character, you will probably have a ton of opportunity to get some photos," Jackie says, leaning closer to me and lowering her voice. "I tell you what—I can't give up my source, but I'll split the payment with you if you get a good picture. I'm sure you could use the money. We all can use some money if we're working this crappy job."

I can't believe what I'm hearing. But I'm also smart

enough to know that I should play nice, because a woman who is willing to screw over innocent actors for money is someone who wouldn't think twice about ruining me, too. So I smile politely and nod. "Sure. I'll, uh, keep an eye out."

CHAPTER 8

Trevor

I film scenes that don't have Andrea's character in them for the next week. We have call times early in the morning before the sun is even up, and I get shuttled to my hotel room late at night, with only enough time to shower and pass out before I have to do it all over again the next day. I've almost forgotten about that cute stand-in actress until I get the call sheet for Monday's filming and see Andrea's name crossed out and Annie's name replaced as the fill in.

I'm not exactly sure how the ballroom scene is supposed to work without the correct actress, but I guess I'm still so new to this industry that I keep forgetting about a little thing called *movie magic*. If the people in charge think they can get it done, who am I to question them?

I creep on Andrea Block's social media feed while I sit for hair and makeup the next morning. The director begged her to stay here in Texas while her arm heals, but she refused and has taken her private jet back home to Cali. She's been posting photos nonstop, showing off her purple cast and soaking up all the love and attention from her fans. She never followed me back. I don't exactly care to have her as a friend, but as a colleague, this is the first time I've worked with someone so stuck up that they don't follow all their other cast members on social media.

"That woman is a real piece of work," my hair stylist says, seeing Andrea's account on my phone as she looks over my shoulder. I click on my home feed to make it look like I'm not creeping on her profile any longer than necessary.

"I don't really know her," I say. "I only saw her at the table read and then the first day of filming when she broke her arm."

The stylist smirks at me from the mirror in front of us as she sprays some kind of product on my hair. "You mean you haven't heard the latest drama with her?"

I lift an eyebrow. "No, but it sounds juicy based on the look on your face."

She snorts out a laugh and glances around, but we're in my trailer and we're alone so there are now prying ears to eavesdrop. "Apparently her agent informed her that they're planning on using the stand-in for the ballroom scene and Andrea threw a fit because that woman is heavier than she is. Don't get me wrong, I think that girl is quite beautiful, but you know, in scientific terms and all, she does look a little bigger. Maybe fifteen pounds bigger? Anyway, Andrea threw an absolute fit saying she didn't want the girl to wear her ballroom scene dress because the fans will think she's gotten curvier when they watch the movie."

My stylist laughs a deep belly laugh. "The director said too bad, it's written in her contract that they can do this very thing, so she'll just have to deal with it. Maybe if she wasn't so horrible to everyone, the director would have taken the time to find a more suitable body double but, oh well. She gets what she deserves."

I smile but say nothing, even though that's the dumbest thing I've ever heard. Annie has an amazing body and Andrea should be happy to have her as a body double. I'm still new in this business, and for all I know, my hair and makeup people are Andrea Block's secret spies, hoping they can get me to say something bad that Andrea will use to ruin my career. You can't trust anyone in Hollywood.

But if I'm being honest to myself, I'm grateful that I get to film some of the scenes with Annie instead of Andrea. Annie is sweet and kind, and Andrea walks around acting like everyone should bow down to her. She's no princess. She's just a highly paid actress, and I'm totally over her crappy attitude.

It's eight in the morning when I arrive at the ballroom set, dressed in a tux with my hair slicked back like I'm super suave. But my character isn't suave, so I have to act like I'm feeling uncomfortable in my fancy clothing. Luckily, I do feel a tad out of place. I'd rather be in jeans and a t-shirt.

I find Annie standing uncomfortably with the director, looking like she'd rather be anywhere else but here. She's been transformed with clothing, hair, and makeup, just like I have, but she cleans up so much better than I ever could. She's absolutely stunning in a maroon silky gown that clings to her curves. Her "Andrea" wig covers her long black hair, but I bet she'd look amazing in her natural hair.

My first thought is that Andrea Block should be sending Annie a thank you card for making her character look so incredibly sexy in that gown. I can't stop staring, and I need to stop staring—it's unprofessional.

A crew member rushes up to Annie and begins covering her face in little white dots—then I realize what form of movie magic they're using today. The dots on her face will make it so that they can CGI Andrea's face into the scene later on. Clever.

"Good morning," I say when I approach Annie and all the crew members around her. My director, Paul, says something back, probably a good morning, but I don't hear it. I'm just looking at Annie. My brain can't seem to focus on anything else.

"I'm going to puke," she says, her eyes fearful and anxious as she looks into mine.

"Really?" a crew member next to her asks, a look of fear on her face.

Annie shakes her head. "No, I don't think so. I'm just... really nervous."

Paul puts a hand on her shoulder. "Don't be. You have no speaking lines. You're just going to dance with Trevor here, and all our shots will be from the side of your face only. Just pretend you're Andrea, and you'll be fine." He pats her shoulder once, then walks off.

She gulps. "I am not Andrea. I'm not even close to being Andrea. I never even tried out for a play in school!"

I chuckle. "Film is nothing like school plays, so you're not missing out. Have you read the script?"

She nods. The ballroom dancing scene will be part of a montage scene on the film, where it shows slow-motion clips of us dancing over voiceovers and flashbacks of the rest of the movie. There's not much talking, and not much to do but dance.

"We've got this," I say, giving her a professional smile, as opposed to the smile I wish I could give her. The *you are so beautiful it makes my insides hurt* smile. If I weren't famous and she was just some woman I met in my regular life, I'd give her the second smile. But that's not our situation and I have to hold it together here.

When the scene begins, a beautiful slow song plays over the ballroom's speakers. It's not the same song that will be in the movie because those sound effects will be added later on, but this music is for our benefit so we know what tempo we're dancing to. The director gives out a few more directions to the extras—all couples who are supposed to see us dancing and then slowly move to the edge of the room, giving the romantic couple a moment to themselves while everyone watches on adoringly.

For now, Annie and I are standing in the middle of the extras, two cameras on either side of us. The director yells, "Action!"

I slide my hands around her waist and pull her close. She smiles up at me, a nervous smile that I wish I could turn into a happy smile with just a quick look—

but she remains nervous over the next minute or two. We dance—I lead and she follows—while surrounded by all these extras.

When the music gets louder, it's the extras' clue to take notice of the romantic couple and start backing away. I hold Annie close, doing the actor thing of pretending I'm my character, and she's Andrea's character, but even though I look professional on the outside, I'm internally thinking about how dang beautiful she is.

Even with her face covered in white plastic dots, she's striking. Her slender nose, and heart-shaped face, and adorably cute eyes that keep flickering up to mine nervously.

I breathe her in, holding tightly to her back, my hand slippery on the silk fabric as I spin her around, dancing to the song.

"Cut!"

The music stops and so do we.

"Let's take it from the top," the director calls out.

"What did I do wrong?" Annie asks him.

"Nothing, you were great."

She turns to me, fear in her eyes as the extras move back into position.

"It's a movie," I whisper. "We often have to do the same thing over and over."

She draws in a deep breath. "Okay."

I smile, my hand slipping down to take hers. "You're doing great. Just breathe."

"I'm trying," she says with a little chuckle. Then we begin again.

Again, and again, I sweep her into my arms, hug her close, smell the light floral scent of her perfume, and look deep into her beautiful eyes.

The makeup crew powders our faces between takes, and then we start again.

After a couple of hours, I've been dancing with this woman so much it feels like second nature. I'm no longer leading the dance—we are in sync, moving rhythmically to each other's bodies, getting lost in each other's eyes.

At least that's what it feels like to me.

Annie seems more at ease. Like she's no longer in fear of puking or passing out. But as for her feelings about me? I don't know if she's just acting or what. But every time we get to the part where the extras back away and it's just us, she looks up at me through her eyelashes and her cheeks turn a little bit pink and I feel like this moment is just for us. Every single time we do it, it feels like the first time. I'll never tire of dancing with her—if anything, I'm growing addicted to it.

"Perfection!" the director calls out on his megaphone. "Absolute perfection."

He hasn't cut the scene yet, so we keep dancing, keep staring into each other's eyes. This is the kind of scene where he can give us stage directions because the sound won't be used for the final film.

Then he yells, "Now let's seal this moment with a kiss!"

Internally, my eyes widen with surprise. But on the outside, my actor self has been trained against reacting to my thoughts—that's an easy way to ruin a scene. I tip my head down a bit so it looks like we're about to kiss, the same way Andrea had said we'd pretend to kiss since she didn't want to actually kiss until it was necessary.

But Annie must not have gotten the memo because she slides her hands around my neck and smirks just a tiny bit before she kisses me.

My entire body lights up.

I pull her closer, deepening the kiss, unsure what's acting and what's just pure primal urges to kiss this beautiful woman.

She kisses me back too, her mouth feeling urgent on mine, her breaths short gasps. Oh no... no, no, no. I can't do this. I can feel the desire rising in me, the feelings that scream *you have a crush on her*, in the back of my mind. This is no fake acting kiss.

This is the real deal. And I have to stop it before it goes too far. *Stop this,* I tell myself. *Pull away and end the kiss, you fool!*

Then a crashing sound fills the crowded ballroom and someone screams in pain.

I wasn't able to pull away from the kiss, but nature just did it for me.

CHAPTER 9

Annie

"My hand!" someone yells as chaos erupts in the ballroom.

Someone is very clearly hurt, crying in pain, and needing assistance. I am a nurse. Helping hurt people is literally my best skillset. And yet, it takes me several shell-shocked seconds to finally blink and come back to reality and realize what's going on around me.

I blink and look around, coming back slowly from that kiss.

That kiss!

Whoa. If kissing Trevor Owens like that is part of being an actress, maybe I should quit my nursing career and move to Hollywood. That was the most incredible kiss I've ever experienced in my entire life. It was powerful enough to make me forget about the newly formed blisters on my heels from spending hours dancing around in these uncomfortable shoes the costume designer put me in. That kiss made me forget every single thing in the world except for Trevor, and me, and our lips, and the electricity bursting through us.

Mentally, I yell at myself. *Get it together, Annie!*

I rush off the dance floor toward the sound of the shrieks, pushing extras aside as I drop to the carpeted flooring in front of the woman who is screaming for help. She's wearing rugged, ripped up and dirty jeans, sneakers, and a black t-shirt with the word CREW on it.

Taking in the scene quickly, it's easy to see what happened. She had been standing on the nearby ladder, replacing a light bulb, when she leaned too far, the ladder slipped, and she fell. It was just a few feet to the floor, but the bulb in her hand shattered and cut her palm. Blood is everywhere.

"It hurts!" she yells to no one in particular, holding her hand out while blood spills everywhere.

"It'll be okay," I say, touching her knee and offering her a small smile. A panicking patient is never good, so anything I can do to calm her down will help everyone out.

I look back toward the first adult who makes eye contact with me. "You need to call an ambulance."

"There's a golf cart just outside," another crew member says. "We can take her to the medical tent."

"I need something to stop the bleeding," I say, looking around. "Something clean."

I don't know where Trevor came from, but suddenly he's grabbing a box from a nearby coffee cart and pulling out a brand new cloth napkin from it. "Will this work?"

Seeing him, his eyes on mine, brings back tingles of desire that roar to life in my stomach and wrap around my throat, making me feel woozy and delighted at the same time. Whoa, this is bad. I take a deep breath and nod, reaching out my hand for the napkin.

I wrap it around the woman's bleeding palm as tightly as I can, then I tuck the end into the top of it, securing it in place "Hold it up high," I instruct, lifting her hand high as Trevor and I help her stand.

"Am I going to bleed out and die?" she says, her words strangled with fear and sobs.

"No, you'll be okay." I shake my head. "You're going to need stitches, though."

Her eyes squeeze shut at the thought. I hold her damaged hand in the air and wrap my arm around her side as the people move out of the way for us to get outside to the golf cart.

I hear a familiar voice curse out loud, then I see the person talking. It's the costume woman who helped me get into this dress. "We only have one of these dresses in your size!"

She fusses about, brushing imaginary dirt off it. "You shouldn't be doing any of this," she complains, following us outside. "You can't damage this dress."

I feel bad, but emergency circumstances overrule her.

"If there's an injured person, I have to help," I explain.

"We have medical people on staff for that," she says back, frowning as she looks me up and down. "You're just an actress."

"Actually, I'm a nurse," I say.

"Are you really?" the injured woman says. It's the first time she's talked normally since hurting herself.

I smile. "Yep. Licensed in the state of Texas."

She breathes a quick sigh of relief. "I'm glad you're here."

I feel Trevor's eyes on me as we walk, the three of us, toward a golf cart driven by a paramedic. I give him a brief description of the injury and he takes over.

"Thank you," the woman calls out to me as she

climbs into the golf cart. I wave at her as she's taken away in the golf cart.

"Let's get back inside," Trevor says, lightly touching my back for a brief moment. But even that slight touch lights up my insides. He frowns. "The show must go on."

"Right," I say, glancing back toward the Lake Sterling banquet hall. It's a real venue for real people, but the film crew has temporarily rented out the entire space.

"I know you're new at this, so I'll warn you that you're probably about to be yelled at," he says as we walk the short distance toward the doors.

"What do you mean?" All of a sudden my cheeks feel hot, because the only reason I can think of for getting yelled at is that a few minutes ago before the light bulb injury, I was literally kissing Trevor Owens. The star of the film. And I was enjoying it a little too much.

Or maybe a lot too much.

And I'm not an actress—I'm just an extra. Just a body double for the real thing, the beautiful, stunning, super talented actress who is *supposed* to be kissing Trevor Owens on that dance floor. Oh gosh. I'm gonna be sick.

"You can't exactly run off set to tend to someone's

wounds," he says, holding the giant glass door open for me. "You're the main character in that scene. Well, me and you, but yeah. We can't leave, even if we have good intentions. Filming doesn't stop until the director says so."

I draw in air through my teeth. "Right. Okay."

Trevor's predictions come true. The director gives me quite a talking to when we return inside, but it's nothing I haven't had to handle from irate nursing managers or the occasional doctor who is upset that I can't read his mind.

I'm told that while I'm an extra, I'm an important extra because I'm filling in for the most important cast member. But the director's lecture only lasts a couple of minutes before he's pulled into another direction by other crew members.

Finally, they announce that due to all the shattered glass and blood, they're going to wrap up filming for the day and we'll all start fresh tomorrow at seven in the morning.

I breathe a sigh of relief. I need to rest my poor feet. And my poor brain. Maybe my brain needs the most rest because it's been replaying that kiss nonstop in my head this whole time.

I chew on the inside of my lip as I walk away from the set, grateful that someone else is talking to Trevor. I don't think I can deal with looking into his eyes right now. It all just brings me back to that incredible kiss.

The costume designer—I feel bad calling her that but I can't remember anyone's names because there are so many people on set—sweeps me away to Andrea Block's costume trailer to make sure she gets her dress back. I slip out of it, standing nearly naked as I look around, only to realize I have no idea where my clothes are. I'd put them on a shelf before changing into the dress earlier. I wait several minutes, but no one comes back, so I steal a clean robe from a rack of robes and slip it on, tying the strap tightly around my waist.

I text Julie to let her know I'm coming home early...as soon as I've found my real clothes.

> **Julie:** oops... I told Max you'd be gone all day so we went to the city to do some shopping and get dinner. So you'll be alone... sorry!

I blow a raspberry as I read her text, but I type out a nice reply.

> **Me:** No worries! I'll just hang out until you're back.

After the day I've had, maybe it's best if I go take a

hot shower to sear out the memory of Trevor's kiss from my mind and then crash on Julie's couch and watch TV.

I open the door to the costume trailer and step out, almost crashing directly into the one person I'm trying to forget.

"Trevor!" my voice sounds like a startled mouse. I swallow. "Hi."

CHAPTER 10

Trevor

"Hello."

Annie looks like a deer caught in the headlights when she sees me. I guess I was standing here kind of close, but that's because I was about to knock on the trailer door to see if she's in there. I take a step back.

"I see Miriam finally got her dress back."

Annie rolls her eyes. "I put her precious dress back on the hanger but I don't know where my own clothes are so I had to steal this robe, which I'm sure will be yet another thing I get yelled at for."

"Nah, I have a million accidentally stolen robes," I say. "They don't keep track of the robes, just the clothes that appear on camera."

"Well, that's good I guess, but I'd still like to know

where my real clothes are. I found my bag in there where I'd left it, but not the clothes."

"I'll help you find them," I say. Movement to the right catches my attention. I'm pretty sure it's just some extras taking a walk, but paranoia always gets me on outdoor film sets. Paparazzi lurk everywhere, even occasionally managing to sneak into places where they aren't allowed. "Come on," I say, motioning for her to follow me three trailers down.

My name is on the door. It's such a small thing but it means so much, as someone who had only once dreamed of being a movie star as a way to earn money. Now I have my own trailer. My life isn't exactly the way I want it to be, but it's not bad. My name is on the trailer door after all.

Annie hesitates when I open it.

"Am I allowed in there?"

"Why wouldn't you be?" I ask.

She bites her lip. "I'm not allowed in the craft services tent. I'm not supposed to touch any of Andrea Block's character stuff unless someone tells me to. I can't leave a scene to go help someone who's injured. I'm already in trouble all the time, so I don't want to get yelled at for going into an actor's trailer."

"It's my trailer so I can do what I want with it," I

say, giving her a smile as I hold open the door. "You're my guest."

She steps inside, the look of awe on her face reminding me of the first time I walked in a trailer myself. It's really just a slightly fancier motorhome, but it's still cool. This film's budget isn't even that great compared to other movies, but the trailer is still fit for a movie star. It's filled with plush seating, a giant TV, snacks, and other amenities that help make it feel like home.

"Wow," she says, wandering down the narrow hallway that leads to the small bedroom. Worry creeps up my spine at the sudden fear that I left a pair of boxers on the floor like the slob I am. But she turns around and walks back before going into the more private area of the trailer, so she doesn't see anything embarrassing.

"Flowers?" she says, reaching out and touching the petals of the fresh bouquet on the dining table. She playfully narrows her eyes at me. "Does someone have a secret admirer?"

I snort out a laugh. "There are fresh flowers delivered every couple of days. I think the crew does it?"

"Wait, it you don't specifically know where they come from?" she says, eyes wide. "Maybe it is a secret admirer. Or a creepy stalker."

"That would explain why they come with a note that says *I'm watching you*," I joke.

This gets a smile from her. Her cheeks turn a light shade of pink and then she looks back at the flowers, leaning in to smell them.

"I'll text the lead crew member," I say, tearing my gaze from her to look at my phone. "I'll make sure they find your clothes."

"Thanks." She sits at the small table, neatly clasping her hands in her lap. I notice she has really good posture, her shoulders straight and back, and I wonder if it's because she's a nurse. Are nurses known for having good posture?

"So how are you liking the gig so far?" I ask. I have to say something, have to keep up a boring conversation about boring things, or I'll go back to thinking of that kiss we shared in the ballroom.

"It's... unusual," she says after a moment of thought. "I have no idea what I'm doing, and I kind of want to quit, but I never break a commitment if I can help it, so..." She shrugs. "I guess I'm here for the two months."

"Why would you want to quit?" I ask, looking at the flowers, which are also beautiful, but in a different way.

She draws in a deep breath. "No offense, but acting

sucks."

I can't help but laugh. "No offense taken."

"I really hope one of my job applications comes through soon. I need to get my life back together."

"What happened to your life to make it not be together?" I ask. I hope that string of word vomit makes sense. To be honest, being in the same room with this gorgeous woman does crazy things to me. And the memories of kissing her less than an hour ago is doing even more crazy things to me.

"Oh that's a long, boring, pathetic story," she says. "Trust me, a big movie star like you would be so bored by the details."

"I'm not a big movie star," I say, casually shrugging off the statement.

She snorts. "Okay, maybe you're not like, Chris Evans yet, but you're going to be some day. Everyone loves you. Oh, speaking of..." She looks over the top of the flowers at me, a suddenly bashful expression on her face. "I know I sound like a total loser right now but, my best friend, and my little cousins, and—let's face it —my mom, would freak out if I sent them a picture of a famous movie star...they would think it's so cool." She bites her lip and holds up her phone. "Would you maybe... let me take a photo of you?"

Even after a few years of being an actor, it still

blows my mind that people get excited to meet me. It's a cool feeling. And it's surreal. And it makes me wonder what the rest of my life will be like. Do I really want this kind of fame forever? No... but it's okay for now. I don't mind taking photos with fans, especially when they're polite about it.

"I'll do you one even better," I say, motioning for her to come over to my side of the table. "Come get in the picture with me."

She grins and walks over, bringing the scent of her perfume with her. I slide over on the small pleather bench seat to make room for her, but she doesn't sit. She just kind of kneels down a bit so that we're both in the picture. Only her arm is shorter than mine so she can't hold the phone out very far.

"I'll do it," I say, taking her phone and holding it out to capture the perfect selfie of us. I snap a couple of pictures—if there's one thing I've learned about taking pictures with fans it's that they always want a few to choose from.

"Hold on, I need to get closer so you can't see my entire robe," she says. "Makes me look like a hobo slob without real clothes on."

She lowers closer to me so that both of our faces are in the frame and you can't really see the details of what she's wearing. She's wobbly as she stands here in the little trailer's dining alcove, balancing in a half-squat. I put an arm around her back to steady her before I snap the picture. I get a couple good ones, and then she slips.

And falls right into my arms. Right into my lap.

I tighten my grip around her back. "Whoa. We can't have you falling and getting injured," I say playfully as I hand her phone back. "The director would lose his mind."

She chuckles too, but her cheeks are flaming red. It feels like mine are warming up, too, and I'm very grateful for my summer tan, hoping it'll hide any evidence that I'm blushing like a schoolgirl.

Time seems to stand still. Annie is sitting in my lap and I don't want her to leave. But of course, we both know she should get up and go back to her side of the table. It's the appropriate thing to do. We are just friends. Friends don't sit on each other's laps.

I take one look into her eyes and I'm undone. I kiss her. Or she kisses me. Or maybe it was some magnetic pull we both felt at the same time and no one is to blame because we're both kissing each other. I breathe her in, feel her soft lips on mine. This time there are no cameras, no witnesses. This time it's even better than before—which I hadn't thought possible because kissing her in that ballroom was magical.

This is somehow better.

She pulls away, jumping to her feet. "I'm sorry! I'm so sorry."

She practically bolts over to the other side of the table, where she sits and covers her mouth with her hands. Her eyes are wide with shock.

"It's okay," I say, not sure what I should say in this moment. My head is still foggy, after all. That was one epic kiss.

"I guess that was just... muscle memory." She swallows, nodding quickly. "Because we had to kiss earlier for the scene and, I guess my lips were just, you know, on automatic muscle memory mode...I'm so sorry. I didn't mean to."

"Yeah, totally. No big deal." I nod in tune with her rambling explanation for what just happened. It's bull crap, and we both know it.

But this is the lie we're choosing to go along with.

So I'm going to make myself believe it.

CHAPTER 11

Annie

Oh my gosh. Oh my gosh.

I can't believe I just kissed him! Again! Without a director telling me to!

What is wrong with me?

He probably thinks I'm some idiotic fangirl and he's going to put a restraining order on me the second I leave his trailer. Maybe he's used to it—I'm sure I'm not the first woman he's ever met who wants to kiss him at inappropriate times. I bet all the women want that. The thought does not comfort me one bit.

I walk over to the front of his trailer where a couch and a TV are and I pretend to be very interested in reading a newspaper on the table just so I have somewhere to look that's not directly into his eyes. They're green, by the way. Dark green that almost seems brown from far away, but up close they're the color of a sunlit forest canopy with little flecks of gold, like a sunset sprinkling in through the leaves.

I swallow. *Stop thinking that!*

He is a famous actor and I am a nobody who doesn't even have a real job or a home right now, so the phrase "out of his league" doesn't even apply here. It's not that I'm out of his league—I'm not even playing the same sport. A man like him would never be interested in a loser like me. Not to mention the whole famous thing.

He's famous. I'm not.

End of story.

There's a sharp knock on his trailer door, which startles me, but seems to put Trevor at ease.

"Your clothes are here," he says, walking over to answer the door. He thanks whoever is on the other side, then turns around, holding out a white plastic bag to me. It has my name written on it. I don't know why someone felt the need to remove my clothes from where I had left them—maybe it's some other movie set rule I don't know about—but at least I have them back now.

"Thanks," I say, grabbing the bag. It's just jeans and a shirt, but for some reason I'm embarrassed to hold a bag of my own clothes in front of him. It's not like there are underwear in there or anything—I'm wearing those, thank you very much.

"You can change clothes here," he says.

My eyes widen at the idea of changing in front of him, but of course that's not what he means. He opens the trailer door and steps out. "I'll give you some privacy."

"That's fine, I'll just go home like this and bring their robe back later."

"It's a long walk to the extra's parking lot and you shouldn't do it in a robe," he says, flashing me a sympathetic smile. "Plus there could be paparazzi and I'm sure you don't want to be on the front page of a gossip magazine as the *mysterious robed woman leaving Trevor Owens' trailer.*"

"Definitely not," I say, feeling scandalized.

He chuckles. "I'm going to grab a snack, so take as long as you need."

When he's gone, I twist the lock on the door just so no random crew members burst in here thinking they'll find Trevor and find me half-naked instead. It only takes a few seconds to change clothes, so Trevor isn't back yet when I finish.

It feels like it'd be rude to just leave without saying goodbye, but I also have no idea how long he'll take. I sit on the couch and check my emails. I have several spam messages from the job websites I signed up for, but no actual job leads yet.

Then I look at my pictures to see how my selfies with Trevor turned out. Even though I technically had to stare at my phone to take the selfie, I was so overcome with anxiety and emotions from being so close to Trevor that I didn't really pay attention to the phone. Just thinking of it now makes my palms feel sweaty and my heart start pounding. I can't believe I fell into his lap.

And then I kissed him.

Once this two month gig is over, I'm sure I'll never see Trevor Owens again. He'll move back to Hollywood and keep being famous and I'll get another nursing job and keep living my boring life. But you know what I'll always have? That kiss. The memories of the kiss.

And of course, the photos.

My jaw drops as I scroll through the picture gallery on my phone. The first couple of photos are okay, but they look like a nervous fan (me) is awkwardly posing for a photo with a handsome actor (him). But then when I lowered myself to fit in the photo better, we look good. Really good. Almost like real friends taking a picture together. Trevor snapped a few photos, which I'm grateful for because I can go through and pick the one that makes me look the least like a doofus. He looks perfect in every single photo.

My smile is a teensy bit goofy and starry-eyed, but I look okay. A little cute, even. Except for the couple of spots on my face that are pink from where I'd pulled off those CGI plastic things they glued to my face. But it's barely noticeable.

And Trevor... oh gosh. The man is a living embodiment of handsome. His smile is gorgeous and easygoing and perfect. Every single shot is perfection, whereas I look awful in some of them and halfway decent in others. How does he do that? Is looking perfect in pictures some kind of skill they teach you at acting school?

With a sigh, I keep scrolling. The last picture was taken on accident, right as I fell into his lap while he was still holding out my phone to take the selfie. I'm a little blurry, my eyes wide as I'm falling. But Trevor— he's looking at me, a split second before he realizes I'm falling. The expression on his face makes my whole body feel flushed. It must just be a trick of the camera —a silly half-second in time that only appears like he's gazing adoringly at me... it can't be real.

But in this photo, he's watching me, a sweet, soft smile on his lips. His eyes are crinkled in the corners as he gazes up at me. If I weren't blurry, it would be a good enough photo to be a promotional poster for the movie. Well, if I weren't blurry and if I I were Andrea Block, the real actress.

He looks like he's in love with me in this photo.

I know it's just a trick of the camera. Just a glitch. Just a weird face he made right before I fell into his lap. But this one image is now the best picture on my phone. I will cherish it forever, even if the emotions in his eyes are just imaginary.

My teeth dig into my bottom lip. I can't wait to show it to Julie!

Oh geez, maybe I am becoming a fangirl.

Disappointment floods my veins when I arrive on set the next day for the second day of filming the ballroom scene after it got cut short yesterday. Andrea Block is here, and Annie is nowhere to be found. There's no time to stand around and chit chat when I get to the set each morning, so I head straight into my hair and makeup trailer to get started, hoping one of the stylists knows what's going on.

"Anyone know why Andrea is back even though her arm is still in a cast?" I ask.

The woman dusting powder across my forehead stops and looks at me, confusion on her face. "She is?"

I shrug. "I saw her walking with her assistant just now."

"Weird," the woman says.

Well, that got me nowhere. After hair and makeup, I put on the gardener costume for today's scenes and head to the set, hoping to see Annie waiting for me, and desperately hoping we're filming that couch make out scene today. In just a short time, Annie has become like a drug to me. Like the coffee so many of my friends can't start their day without.

I don't want to start my day without Annie.

I don't even know her phone number or her last name, but I can't stop thinking about her and I'm so eager to spend time with her again.

And yes, in the back of my mind, there's a part of my subconscious that's screaming at me to shut up and get over her and never think of her again. But I can't just put her out of my mind. It's impossible.

I am not the kind of guy who hooks up with women randomly. I've only ever been interested in a real relationship, which is why I haven't dated in years. Dating feels impossible as an actor. I'm waiting until I quit this job to find a great woman and settle down. I am nowhere close to having enough money to quit acting for good—so why can't I quit Annie?

I quickly learn that we aren't filming the make out scene today. Bummer. The weird thing with movies is that they often film out of order, so while earlier this week we were filming the ballroom scene which is the end of the movie, today we're filming a scene that's right at the start.

This is a scene where I take a coworker to the hospital where Andrea's character is a nurse. Her character and mine are enemies at first, so we bicker and get on each other's nerves in this scene. The hospital we're using is actually an office building that's been staged to look like a hospital.

Everyone is getting ready to begin filming as if everything is normal, but I don't see Annie and it's starting to look like she won't be here today.

The director approaches us smelling like coffee and cigars. "Slight change of plans," he says to the group as a whole. "We'll be using techniques to hide Andrea's cast while filming, so I hope you've all read the script notes I sent over late last night. Let's have a good day, everyone. We'll take it from the top."

Whoops. I didn't read any new script notes because I never checked my email last night or this morning. I spent the whole night in my hotel room thinking about that kiss with Annie and wondering how long I can let myself feel these feelings about a woman I'm not allowed to like or date.

Crew members bring in props to carefully hide Andrea's broken arm, just like how I've seen shows filmed when an actress is pregnant but trying to hide her belly on screen since her character isn't pregnant. It works fairly well. Andrea wears scrubs, her hair tied back in a ponytail, and she holds a pile of linen draped over her cast at the start of the screen.

Then they have her sitting at a desk or standing half-hidden by a doorway... stuff like that. It works well. I say my lines and do each take the same way, changing slightly if the director requests it.

The day drones on for hours. When we break for lunch, I scope out the dozens of people mulling around the fake hospital set, but none of them are Annie.

Finally, I find an empty waiting room at the end of the hall where they're keeping the extras between filming. I glance around the room, ignoring all the excited looks I get from extras who probably think it's cool that the main character is here. I don't see Annie.

I turn to walk away but someone calls my name. I stop, noticing a young woman with light hair waving at me as she walks over.

"Hi, I'm Jackie," she says, smiling up at me the way so many woman have before. She has this hopeful, excited look in her eyes, like the women who run into me in public and beg me to take a picture with them. It's a little unusual to see all this swooning coming from a paid extra, though. They're professionals and they usually act like it.

"Nice to meet you," I say, wondering if she knows Annie.

"What are you doing back here with us extras?" she asks, shifting on her feet so that she's in front of me now and it would be rude if I just ducked around her to leave.

"I was, uh, looking for someone."

"Someone special?" she asks, wiggling her eyebrows. "Are you dating someone, Trevor Owens, and keeping it a secret?" Her voice is playful and joking, but a suspicious feeling creeps up my spine. Sounds like she's hoping to glean any private information she can about me so she can rush off and tell her social media about it. Ugh. I'm so sick of people and their desperation for social media clout.

I chuckle like that's the dumbest idea ever. "Nah, no way. I have no plans to date anyone."

She frowns. "Well, that's just boring. What else is going on with you? Have you talked to Andrea Block lately? What do you think about her?"

Ugh, this woman is annoying. "I have to get back to set," I say, politely stepping around her. "It was nice meeting you."

No, it wasn't, actually. But the last thing I need is

for some extra to go blabbing to a reporter that Trevor Owens is a jerk to crew members. Then I'll get a reputation for being a problematic diva on set, and I don't feel like fielding questions from people on the red carpet about how I'm a jerk. So politeness it is.

Andrea and I film some more, and she never gets any nicer or friendly as the day goes on. She acts like she's better than anyone else here, and that we are all blessed to be in her superior acting presence. In a way, she is better since she's far more famous, but her rude personality really grates on me. I'm not trying to become best friends or anything, but a little friendly conversation never hurt anyone.

In every other film I've been in, you get friendly with the cast members and go out to dinner and stuff each night. With this film, I have Annie and no one else. My nights are lonely. My lunches are boring since she doesn't come to the craft services with me anymore. And now today, she's not even here.

The day goes by, and I do my job, but I'm miserable. This is not good—not for my acting abilities or for my heart, which is aching right now. It's literally aching like I'm some kind of love-sick idiot.

I barely even know this woman! Why am I reacting this way to not having her near me?

Once shooting is wrapped up for the day, I find the director getting another refill of coffee at craft services.

"So is Andrea back for good?" I ask casually. I know I could have asked the actress myself, but she's not very friendly. As soon as the cameras stop rolling after each take, she walks away to be with her assistant, not talking to anyone else. Andrea Block is the very definition of stuck up.

Paul looks at me with a tight-lipped expression my dad has given me a million times in my life. "You didn't read the email, did you?"

I stumble over words of denial and then I stop and shrug. "I never saw it, sorry."

He rolls his eyes. "It was going to cost too much to CGI her face into the film, so she either had to accept less pay or come back to work. She chose the work, but she and her agent are not too happy with me. Luckily, the network has her in a three-film contract so she can't break it without losing even more money."

He pours an obscene amount of sugar into his coffee and then looks up at me, a defeated expression on his face that tells me he'd much rather be directing big blockbuster movies and not made-for-TV romances. "We already got the major kiss scene in the ballroom done, so everything else should be easy enough to film while hiding her cast. They're replacing the white cast with a flesh-colored cast tonight so it'll blend in even better if we miss hiding it in some spots. Then they're changing her wardrobe to include long sleeves."

"So no more body double?" I ask.

"Nah," he says, taking a sip of his coffee. "It's a good thing too," he says with a snort, "because that woman was sweet and all, but she's a terrible actress."

My hopes are crushed into pieces so small they disperse through my chest cavity and make everything hurt. I haven't been this disappointed in, well, ever. When I lost out on the opportunity to audition for a superhero movie last month, I was devastated. But this feels worse than that. This feels like I've just missed out on an amazing opportunity. On an amazing woman.

I don't even know how to call her or get in touch with her.

I take a deep breath, pour myself a cup of coffee and tell myself to get over it. I can't go falling in love with extras. I know this. As long as I'm a movie star, I can't go falling in love with anyone.

So instead of feeling sad and moping around all day, I should be grateful that life has taken Annie out of the picture because it makes everything easier if I'm not falling in love with someone I shouldn't date.

I'm not grateful, but I should be.

CHAPTER 13

Annie

When I was a kid, my mom taught me that it was easier to just rip off the bandage from my skinned knee than to slowly peel at it. As a kid, I had assumed that slowly peeling away the sticky bandage would limit the pain, but it took so long and it only stretched out the pain. Using my mom's advice, I grabbed the bandage, closed my eyes, and ripped it off instantly. It stung, but the pain was over in a split second.

It's really easy to do that with a skinned knee. But in real life, it's so much harder to rip painful things out of your life. For example, I had gotten used to going to work at the film set every day, anxiously hoping to see Trevor. I knew it was pointless to have a crush on this man because he's a celebrity. Crushing on him makes me just one of a million women who crush on him.

But I also didn't care, because to be perfectly honest, my life has been stressful lately. Crushing on Trevor was the one fun part.

I had assumed I would have two months to slowly peel off the pain of losing Trevor when the film finishes and he goes back to his fancy Hollywood life. It was just a silly crush. I had two months to bask in it.

Nope!

Andrea Block came back to work early and I get a call at five in the morning from the casting director's assistant telling me I'm no longer needed.

"Don't worry," she says, somehow managing to sound cheerful and also in a hurry to get off the phone with me. "Your contract was for eight weeks, so you'll be paid the full amount. Thanks for all your great work."

I barely get out a reply before she ends the call and I'm left sitting up on my futon bed in the spare room/office of Julie's house. It's early, and I should just go back to sleep since I don't have to go to work today, but now I'm bummed and I don't feel tired.

Trevor was supposed to be a slow, painful removal. And now he just got ripped out of my life. Somehow, the easier option feels like it hurts more.

I draw in a deep breath and straighten my shoulders. Back at my old job, my coworker Shelby was this fitness guru who was obsessed with wellness and yoga and stuff. Every time she'd walk by me she'd tap on my spine just between my shoulders and say, "Straighten that back, Annie!"

I'd fix my posture for her, then slump back down once she left the room. But as much as I don't want to admit it, there's some merit in her obsession with good posture. I feel a little bit braver when I sit up straighter. I feel a little bit more in control of my life. With my back straight, there's not as much room for my heart to hurt so much.

Since I can't sleep, and even lying in bed and closing my eyes is no fun because my brain keeps making me think of kissing Trevor, I decide to get up. I've applied for over a hundred jobs so far, and I have email alerts that let me know if anything new is posted, so there's nothing really for me to do besides go outside.

The air is crisp and perfect this early in the morning. With my favorite pair of running shoes on, I walk out Julie's back yard and toward Lake Sterling with plans of getting in an early morning jog.

The jog part lasts about ten minutes and then I'm out of breath and feeling like I'm going to drop dead from all the exertion. Gosh, I'm out of shape. I walk instead, heading in the opposite direction of the film set. They'll be setting up this early in the morning, getting ready to film whatever scenes they're filming today. They've rented out the entire west side of the lake, including the walkways that go around the lake, so it's not like I could get close anyhow. I walk to the east, toward Roger's Diner.

My phone buzzes from the pocket on the thigh of my leggings. My heart leaps in anticipation. Is it Trevor?

I pull out my phone, biting on my bottom lip, only to be extremely disappointed when I see Max's name on the screen. I don't know why I'd hoped it would be Trevor. He doesn't even have my number.

But he is a famous celebrity and if he wanted to get my number, he could have asked the casting director...

I shrug off the thought and see what Julie's boyfriend has messaged me.

Max: hey can you call me as soon as you can without Julie knowing about it?

Well, it's not as good as a text from Trevor, but my curiosity is piqued, that's for sure. I call him.

"Wow, that was fast," he says with a chuckle.

"I'm dying to know why Julie can't know that

we're talking," I say, even though I'm fairly certain I know the reason.

"I'm going to propose," he says.

I let out a little squeak of excitement. "I am so excited!"

"Me too," he says bashfully. "I've been looking for the perfect engagement ring and I've narrowed it down to my three favorites. I was wondering if you could come help me choose the perfect one?"

"Oh my gosh, yes," I say. My best friend deserves the absolute best ring in the entire world and I would love to help make sure she gets it. We decide to meet up at the custom jeweler he's using in two hours. That gives me just enough time to head home, shower the sweat off, and make up an excuse about why I'm going out and why Julie can't come with me.

Luckily, Julie is busy writing her next novel, so she doesn't even ask to come with me when I tell her I'm heading out to run errands. She's also so busy that she doesn't notice how weird I'm acting. I'm trying really hard to play it cool and calm so she doesn't realize something sneaky is happening. I think I pull it off.

I've never seen Max so flustered when we pick out the ring. It's adorable and it makes me long for my own future romance one day. I know in recent years I've basically given up the hope that I'd ever find a man worthy of my time, but now my thoughts are changing. Now, I wish I would find someone like that. Someone like Trevor.

But this isn't about me. It's my best friend's time to shine right now. Max shows me the options and it's easy for me to pick the best one. A gorgeous round solitaire diamond and a platinum band with tiny little diamonds all around it. It's elegant and sparkly and Julie will love it.

"So how are you proposing?" I ask after we've chosen the perfect ring and he finishes paying for it.

"I know Julie will want something simple, so I'm proposing at her house," he says. "On the back porch, actually. It's where we first kissed, so it's sentimental. But I also know that she'll want to celebrate the event, so my plan is to have you and all her friends secretly meet up at the diner. I'll propose, and then—" he swallows. "Assuming she says yes..."

"She will!" I say, lightly punching him in the arm. "She totally will say yes!"

"Assuming she does, I'll tell her we should celebrate at Roger's Diner since she loves the place so much. And when we arrive, I'll have the entire party room filled with her friends and food."

"And decorations!" I say.

He quirks an eyebrow. "Only if you help me with these decorations?"

"Of course. I'll set up the engagement party at the diner—you handle the proposal and I'll make the celebration party perfect."

He grins. "Thanks, Annie. Can you help me invite everyone?"

"Yep," I say, bouncing on my toes while we walk along the sidewalk of the historic shopping center in Sterling. "I'm so excited. Thank you for letting me help."

"Thank you for helping," he says, taking a deep breath. "I'm really excited but I'm scared."

"Don't be scared. She loves you, and she can't wait to be your wife."

He smiles down at me, the muscley carpenter acting all swoony and in love. It's really sweet. True love if you ever saw it.

"You can bring someone, too," he says. "If you're dating someone or whatever. A plus one."

I frown. "Eh... if I happen to meet a handsome man in the next two days, then sure."

He laughs. "Don't give up. I almost did, but then I met Julie."

I hug him goodbye and then head to the nearest coffee

shop so I can load up on caffeine before I start planning this epic proposal celebration party at the diner. He plans to propose tomorrow night, so I'm on a short time frame but I have no doubt that I'll get the party all ready to go in no time at all. I'll recruit the diner's waitstaff to help me. They all adore Julie and will no doubt be excited to help.

"Annie?"

The voice comes from a table at the back of the coffee shop. I turn around and find that girl from the film set... the extra. I think her name is Jackie.

"Oh, hey," I say, smiling at her as I take my coffee from the barista.

"Come sit with me," she says, patting the empty seat next to her.

"I can't stay long. I'm planning a party for my friend," I say. But I sit down anyway because not sitting down would feel rude. "You're not working today?"

She shakes her head. "They didn't call many extras to set today. Hopefully tomorrow." She takes a sip of her iced coffee then wiggles her eyebrows at me. "So how are you, miss-kisses-Trevor-Owens?"

I roll my eyes. "It was just acting."

"You know how many extras would kill to be you?" She sighs. "I would kill to be you, girl. Mmhmm, that man is so sexy."

I laugh. "It was... interesting, that's for sure."

"Speaking of," she says, flashing me a grin that sends a chill down my spine. "Guess who got five grand for this?"

She holds out her phone, showing me a picture of Trevor Owens, shirtless, leaning against the outside of his trailer. He's got a plastic straw hanging out of his mouth while he looks at his phone.

"Someone paid you five thousand dollars for that?" I ask.

She nods eagerly. "Yup. Candid photo on the set of a closed area the real paparazzi can't get to. It's worth money. That's the only shot I've been able to get, though. Hopefully I'll get something better soon."

"If you think that's good, you should see this."

I have no idea what comes over me. Seriously—no idea. But I can't help myself. I take out my phone and pull up the picture. *The* picture.

She takes one look at it—the selfie of Trevor and me in his trailer—and her jaw drops. "Oh my gosh, you *slept with him*!?"

"What? No!" I hiss, trying to keep my voice down. "No, no, nothing like that."

I put the phone on the table face down, just to keep the adorable photo out of my thoughts long enough to form a coherent sentence. "I was just waiting on the crew for something, so he invited me inside and then I asked for a selfie to show my friends."

"Girl, it looks like you're wearing a bathrobe."

"I was," I admit. "But I was waiting on my clothes because they got misplaced. It was that day I had to wear the ballgown."

Jackie is staring at me like she doesn't believe a word I said, so I feel compelled to change her mind. "Seriously, nothing happened."

But technically something happened. The kiss happened.

I shrug the thought away and lie through my teeth. "Nothing happened. It was just a selfie."

She blows out a long breath, shaking her head. "Girl, you could get so much money for that."

"No way. I'm not selling it."

"Your loss," she says with *a tsk.*

The barista calls my name, telling me that the computer system froze and my credit card charge for my coffee didn't go through. Normally I'd be annoyed at a hassle like that, but right now I'm grateful for the change of conversation.

"Be right there," I say, as I dig my credit card out of my purse and go to the counter to pay.

CHAPTER 14

Trevor

Spending all day filming with Andrea Block is exhausting. The woman is so stuck up and full of herself that she ruins the vibe of every room she walks into. I feel like I should win every acting award in existence for the performance I'm doing. This is some high-level acting skill to read my lines and make it look like I'm falling in love with her on screen. The woman is a rude brat. I don't know how her equally famous and rich boyfriend puts up with her.

I'm so exhausted from filming. I miss Annie. And I hate being stuck in my hotel room. On Saturday morning I decide I need to get out of here or I'll lose my mind. I get creative with the clothes in my suitcase and some items from the hotel's gift shop. The gift shop's clearance rack had discount sweatshirts that advertised the thirty-third annual Lake Sterling fishing competition that apparently happened last month. I buy one and match it with a pair of sweatpants. No one who sees me would think I'm a celebrity when I'm wearing a fishing competition sweatshirt... right?

I know it's risky. My manager would tell me not to go out in public if I wanted to stay under the radar. But he's not here, and I'm sick of my hotel room.

I wear a beanie, tucking all my hair up underneath it, then I put on a pair of sunglasses. Does it work to disguise myself? I'm not so sure. But I'm going to risk it anyway.

On the way out my hotel door, I notice a newspaper on the floor, so I pick up and fold it open to the sports page. When someone walks by, I can pretend to be reading the paper. It may not be a fool-proof plan, but it's something and I make it out to the parking lot with no one noticing a thing.

In my rental car, I hit the road. Sterling is such a small town that it really only has one main road and some smaller roads that seemingly lead to nowhere. I cruise around, get bored, then turn back to the small town so I can grab a bite to eat.

The historic main street is charming, with old fashioned iron streetlamps lining the road, antique-looking shops, and lots of small-town flair. My ideal place to stop would be at a small restaurant owned by an old couple who don't watch much TV and have no idea who I am. I drive slowly down the road, keeping an eye out for something like that.

But then I see Annie and my heart skips a beat.

I slow to a crawl in the car while I approach her as she walks on the sidewalk. I lower the car window.

"Hey beautiful, need a ride?"

She jumps, then looks at me, a horrified expression on her face for a quick moment before she realizes that the crazy guy yelling at her from a car is me. Very quickly her fearful expression turns into a grin.

"What are you doing here?" she asks, walking up to my car as I pull over on the side of the road.

I shrug. "I had to get out of that hotel room."

"And you're in a disguise, I see?" She peers down at me from above her sunglasses. "Or are you just one of those celebrities who dresses weird for the sake of it?"

I grin. "I'm trying to blend in."

"No one in Sterling dresses like you, Trevor."

"Is that a good thing or a bad thing?" I ask.

She considers me for a second. "Both."

"You want a ride?" I ask, desperately hoping she agrees.

To my great delight, she does.

My rental car smells like flowers and vanilla when

she slips into the passenger seat. The scent of her immediately brings me back to working with her in front of the cameras. To kissing her in my trailer. Being near Annie always smells nice, and I hadn't realized how much I wanted to be near her again until just this moment.

Maybe my heart didn't have a random desire to cruise around town. Maybe it just wanted to find her.

"So where are you headed?" I ask, trying to play it cool.

"Home, actually." She tucks her hair behind her ears. "I've been running errands all day but I'm done now."

"Your errands don't include tons of shopping bags?" I ask. She's carrying a purse, but nothing else.

"Yes, technically, but I already dropped them off at the diner." She smiles to herself as she gazes out the window. "I've spent the day planning an epic party for tonight. It was way more fun than pretending to be an actress," she says with a grin. "I am not a good actress."

"No," I agree with a chuckle. "But you did well for someone with zero acting training."

"You don't have to humor me," she says. "I know I sucked. That's why they fired me."

"They *fired you*?" I'm about to call up the director personally and chew him out and demand that he hire her back. She's the best extra this industry has ever had. And by best, I mean the most beautiful. But still.

She shrugs. "I guess it wasn't a firing... they just didn't need me anymore. Which is fine, because it's not like that was my dream job or anything, but I hope I find a new job soon."

"Well, I miss you on set," I say, rolling to a stop at a red light. I look over at her, wishing I could take in her beauty in a better way. Like by having her in my arms instead of sitting next to me in a car.

"It was an experience I'll never forget. But I won't be applying for acting jobs ever again," she says with a chuckle. "It's dramatic and stressful."

"Ouch."

"No, I didn't mean you!" She touches my arm and it sends a shiver of heat up my body. "Working with you was fun. I just mean all the hustle and bustle of it. The early call times, getting yelled at by various crew members, losing my clothes... it's crazy."

"Try working alongside Andrea Block," I say with a grimace. "The woman is a nightmare. That's why I went for a drive today... I just had to get out of the hotel and away from the set. I wanted to feel like a regular human for a few hours."

"Well..." she says, peering at me. Then she points. "Turn here. Sorry, forgot to tell you where I live."

I turn. "Well, what?" I ask, wondering what she was about to say. Judging by the way she said it, it was something good.

"I don't know... I thought about inviting you to something, but it might not be your scene."

"What is it?"

"My best friend is getting engaged tonight and we're throwing a party for the happy couple at Roger's Diner. If you wanted to come with me, you could." She shrugs and shakes her head like she immediately regrets asking me. You'd think she just asked me to the prom with how awkward she looks now. "I mean, it's no big deal. Like, I was going to ask you but then I remembered you're a famous celebrity so obviously stupid dinners in small towns is *so not* your idea of a fun night—"

"I'll do it," I say, interrupting her before she talks herself out of inviting me. "I'd love to go."

"Are you sure?" She peers at me while biting her bottom lip. "Turn left," she says. "It's that white house up ahead."

"Is food involved?" I ask.

"Of course."

"And your company?"

"Yes, I'd be with you the whole time."

I grin. "Then it sounds like a perfect night. I'd love to go."

I pull into the parking lot of the little white home she pointed out. It's a small, well-maintained house, filled with small town charm.

"Okay, cool." Annie's nervous grin is adorable. It makes my heart beat faster. She puts a hand on the door handle but doesn't open it yet. "Should I... call your assistant or something and give you the address?"

I quirk an eyebrow.

"I don't know!" she says with a shrug. "How are you supposed to contact celebrities? It's weird. I don't know how it works."

"Annie, I'm just a regular guy," I say, my voice soft. I want her to see me that way, like any other guy she knows. I know it's not entirely true, but I wish it was. I wish we were just two people who could fall in love and live happily together. "I know where you live now since I'm here in your driveway, so what time should I pick you up?"

"Um, seven?"

"I'll be here."

CHAPTER 15

Annie

I'm so filled with secrets I'm about to burst. The biggest secret of all—that my best friend is about to get engaged—is swelling around inside my ribcage making me feel almost sick with excitement. And then the second secret is Trevor. Is it technically a date if you invite a man to a surprise engagement party? And that man is a celebrity? And you've kissed him?

I clench my teeth together to stop myself from squealing out in excitement. Of course it's not a date... or maybe, technically, it *is* a date, but it's not like this can go anywhere. Trevor Owens is a famous celebrity. He doesn't even live in here in Sterling. Now that I think about it, I don't even live here in Sterling. I'm just couch-surfing at Julie's until I figure out my life. Moving to Hollywood in the hopes that Trevor would date me is definitely not the plan. I may be stupid when it comes to gazing into his gorgeous golden eyes, but I'm not stupid enough to think I can chase after a celebrity and make him like me. Nope. Not that stupid.

I take a deep breath. Trevor dropped me off at Julie's house half an hour ago. She's in her office writing her next book and didn't even notice the strange car in the driveway, or how we stayed there talking for several minutes before I finally walked inside. Luckily, when Julie is in her "writing zone" she's pretty much blind to the world going on around her.

I use this to my advantage as the day goes on, staying in the living room on my computer, acting like I'm just looking for jobs. I can't be suspicious. I can't look like I'm hiding something. This proposal needs to be a total surprise. Max and I have planned it out, so when he comes over after work to hang out, it's so simple and normal that Julie doesn't even question it.

Then when they go to the back porch under the lights that reflect off the lake, making everything gorgeous and romantic, Julie has no idea what's about to happen. But I do. And I'm already in position.

Hidden by the shadows, I'm standing off to the side of the porch, camera in hand and already recording, so that when Max drops down to one knee and proposes, I've got it all on film. Julie's startled gasp, her excited *yes*, and the way her jaw drops when he slides the ring on her finger. I capture it all. My heart is so full, it's about to burst.

A few moments later, Max reveals that I've been here the whole time and Julie's jaw drops again. "You got this on camera?" she says, happy tears rolling down her face.

"Yep," I say, holding up my phone. "It's the most adorably romantic thing I've ever seen."

"I can't believe you two planned this so secretly!" she says, pulling me into a hug. When we part, she looks at her ring, her eyes beaming with happiness. I knew we chose the perfect ring for her, and seeing her happiness now only confirms that.

"How about we celebrate with some dinner?" Max says as if he just thought of the idea. "Roger's Diner?"

"Yes, absolutely," Julie says, bouncing on her toes. "I need to go get dressed first. I can't be showing off this gorgeous ring in the ugly clothes I'm wearing now."

I breathe a quick sigh of relief. Julie wanting to change clothes was part of the plan.

"I'm gonna head out early and make sure to get us the good table that overlooks the water," I say. This is also part of the plan—extracting myself quickly so I can make sure the surprise party is all set up when they arrive. Max winks at me without Julie noticing, and I grab my purse and head outside.

Luckily, Trevor is exactly on time. His rental car rolls into the driveway the moment I step out the front door. Having my own personal celebrity escort was not part of the plan, but I'm not complaining... this actually makes the entire night better.

"How'd the proposal go?" he asks, stepping out of his car as I walk up to it.

"It was perfection."

He walks over to my side and opens my door, a gentlemanly act I'm aware of in a general sense, but I'm pretty sure no man has ever opened my door for me before. The gesture makes my heart feel all warm inside.

"You'll have to tell me all about it," he says, grinning at me before shutting the door.

I watch him walk back around to his side. He looks like a freaking magazine model in designer jeans, a blue shirt, and a black blazer on top of it. Everything is all crisp, clean lines with a muscular undertone. Holy cow he looks amazing. I'm wearing a simple black cocktail dress and some silver sparkly flats. Fancy by my standards, but I feel like a pile of garbage compared to him.

It's a very short drive to the diner, and before I know it, we're here. And I'm suddenly realizing that I'm about to walk into the party with a celebrity by my side.

"Umm," I say, looking over at the insanely gorgeous man next to me.

"What's wrong?"

"You're not wearing a disguise, and I just realized that you might be the center of attention tonight…" I reach for my phone. "I have an idea."

I call the diner and ask for Clare, who is Julie's favorite waitress who also happens to be helping me set up the surprise dinner party. I explain to her that I'm bringing Trevor Owens. After she expresses her excitement over meeting him, I tell her my fears.

"I don't want his celebrity status to detract from the party tonight," I say, watching him as he watches me from his driver's seat. "Is everyone already there?"

"Yep, we're all here waiting to surprise the happy couple."

"Do you think you could tell everyone that Trevor is coming and that they need to be cool and respectful and not like, freak out about it?"

She chuckles. "I'll do that, but you shouldn't worry. Julie's friends here in Sterling are mostly older people who don't really care about stuff like that. Plus,

I've got the party room sectioned off, and all the buffet tables on the patio are blocking the public from wandering into your section, so we can sit you and him in the back corner. No other restaurant guests will notice him, I promise."

"You're the best," I say.

"Walk around the back by the catering van. I can sneak you inside the employee's door and no one will notice you get here."

I grin, then relay all the information to Trevor, who nods. "That's really thoughtful of you, Annie. I appreciate it."

We sit here in his car, shrouded by darkness, and I watch him, see the anxiety on his features, and the way he tries to hide it. "It must be exhausting being a celebrity," I ponder out loud.

He runs a hand through his caramel-colored hair. "You have no idea."

In this moment, my heart hurts for him. Sure he's rich and famous and good looking, but it also means he misses out on just regular things like engagement parties that the rest of us can go to without thinking about. And in this realization, I also have to take a step back from my crush on him. I realize that the silly crush is just that—a silly, pointless crush. I can't date a man like Trevor. He's too famous. It just wouldn't work.

My chest aches. I know the reality and yet, here I am still giddy deep down inside because I want to enjoy this date as if it were real, as if it could lead to something romantic and powerful and everlasting. A knot rises in my chest. This date won't lead to anything —but at least I can enjoy the night. One night of fantasy fun, then it's back to reality for me.

I think Roger's Diner has done a better job of catering to a celebrity than any place in Hollywood ever has. And I don't mean that in an arrogant way. Annie introduces me to a woman named Clare who slips us into the employee's entrance and takes us to a table on the back patio that's in the far corner of the restaurant's large outdoor seating area. She doesn't make a big deal about me, and no one else does, either. It's really refreshing feeling like the old days before I started acting and people started to recognize me.

I don't know the happy couple being honored tonight, but it's still a joy to watch them enter into the private party area of the restaurant to a chorus of their friends all congratulating them. Over the past few years, I've been to several parties to celebrate people's achievements and life events, but none of them were like this. Those Hollywood parties are filled with glitz and glamour and people pretending to be friends while snidely making rude comments about each other behind closed doors. Those parties are exhausting. This party is fun, relaxed, and easygoing.

We are treated to dinner that's brought out by servers all wearing matching shirts that say *Congrats Max & Julie!* Annie gasps when she sees them.

"The shirts look so great!"

"So you planned this whole thing?" I ask her after a server brings us the first course of a Caesar salad.

"I had help from Clare," she says, taking the silverware from the cloth napkin and spreading the napkin on her lap. "I think it turned out pretty good for being such a short notice. Julie looks thrilled, and that's all I could have hoped for."

I glance over at the happy couple who are making their way around to each table, giving out hugs and showing off the engagement ring. When they make their way toward us, Annie's friend is beaming from ear to ear. She looks like the picture-perfect example of someone in love.

"I can't believe you did this," Julie says to Annie.

Annie shrugs playfully, like it's no big deal. "You're

my best friend, and I'm so excited that you're engaged now."

"I'm engaged!" Julie says. They both laugh and then hug each other.

Julie glances at me, still smiling, but in a curious way.

"Hello," I say, standing up and holding out my hand. "I'm Trevor."

"Julie," she says. "And this is my fiancé, Max."

"Oooh, fiancé," Annie says, sing-songing the word.

"I know," Julie says. "I get to call him my fiancé now!"

Max shakes my hand. "Nice to meet you, man."

"You too," I say.

Annie puts a hand on her best friend's arm. "Have you eaten yet? I ordered all your favorite things, and we're getting milkshakes and a chocolate fondue for dessert, so you better make sure you don't forget to eat."

"Ooooooh," Julie says, eyes wide with delight. She turns to her fiancé. "Babe, we've done enough talking. Let's go eat."

The second course is brought out soon after, and the food is so good that Annie and I get caught up eating and don't talk for a few minutes. It's a beautiful night outside. Perfect weather for outdoor eating. The lake beyond the restaurant patio is sparkly underneath the restaurant lights. Relaxing music plays from speakers overhead, and all around us people are having a good time enjoying a delicious meal. This is by far my favorite night in Texas.

I can't stop staring at Annie while we sit together, tucked away in the corner. It almost feels like we're all alone even though we're technically surrounded by people. She's gorgeous in a simple black dress, her long hair looking so silky smooth that I want to run my fingers through it.

I ask her about her best friend, and she tells me all about their years-long friendship. Then she talks about how she used to work in Dallas and how Julie took her in when she lost her job. I really admire that she doesn't give up and doesn't fall apart when things go wrong. Annie is a survivor. She's strong and incredible and I'm so lucky to have met her.

And kissed her.

If I'm being honest, everything about this little surprise party is more romantic than any movie I've ever been in. Love is in the air, you could say. Happiness is everywhere. Or maybe that's just how I feel when I'm around her. She looks so beautiful tonight. The overhead string lights cast an angelic glow on her skin, and her smile lights me up so much that I keep saying funny things just to see her smile again.

I really hope I get another kiss tonight.

"You don't always feel like a celebrity," Annie says, breaking the silence. Her lips form the softest but thoughtful smile.

"What do you mean?"

"Sometimes you just feel like a real man."

"I am a real man." I knock on my chest as if proving that I'm real and not some holographic projection.

She giggles, then rolls her eyes and reaches for her sweet tea. "I just mean sometimes, like right now, you just feel like a regular man in a regular small town, on a date with a regular lady like me. I have to constantly remind myself that you're none of those things."

A pain twists in my gut. "I am those things... This is a small town, and I'm on a date with you."

Her lips form a flat smile as she gazes past me, out at the water. "Yeah, but we both know this isn't a real date." She wiggles her fingers in the air. *"You're a celebrity."*

I stare at her, waiting until her eyes rise up and catch mine. How is it possible to feel so happy and yet so sad at the same time?

"You make me want to quit acting," I say.

Her eyes widen. Mine do too, for that matter.

Did I really just say that?

"Um… what?" she says, her voice barely a whisper.

Every instinct I have tells me to quickly backtrack over my words, deny what I just said, laugh, and make it a joke. That would be the right thing to do—the safe thing. The career-saving thing. Just deny it and move on with my life, leaving this beautiful woman here in a small town where I found her.

Sometimes my instincts are right, but sometimes they are just plain wrong. Sure, logically speaking, the correct thing for me to do is to let Annie go and never see her again. But my heart has taken over my body, sitting itself in the driver's seat and demanding that it be in control for once.

"I really like you," I say, my voice also a whisper. "But…"

"I know," she says before I can finish my sentence. "But it doesn't matter because you're an actor with a big fancy life and I'm a small town girl."

She smiles and pats my hand before picking up her fork again. "It's fine, Trevor. I mean, I had a little crush on you too, but that's over. It's no big deal. Let's just have fun tonight, okay?"

My chest constricts. Everything she just said was

wrong. I was going to say: *I really like you but I'm not sure how you feel about me.*

I guess it's good that she interrupted me because now I don't have to make a total fool of myself. Now I realize that she doesn't feel the same for me, that it was just a short-lived crush for her, and not a life-changing love like what I feel.

I take a breath and force all those years of acting classes to come together right now and help me pretend that I agree with her. That I totally feel the same way.

"Yeah," I say, keeping my voice calm and level. "Let's just have fun tonight."

CHAPTER 17

Annie

I'm proud of myself for saying what needed to be said. For clearing the air and metaphorically pulling all the mud out of the water so that I could see clearly again. I had to say something. I just couldn't stop thinking about how this whole night with Trevor was basically a date that I had asked him on. Dates have implications... Dates are a romantic event between two people who like each other and have romantic intentions.

I had to nip that in the bud immediately, or else my stupid heart would have spent the entire night swooning over this impossibly gorgeous man. My lips would suffer with that tingle of desire from wanting to kiss him again. I wouldn't be able to focus on anything all night if I'd kept up with the pretense that this is a date. So I did what I had to do. I told him we're just friends, and this night is just for fun, and it means nothing.

Technically, I lied when I told him I no longer have a crush on him, but that's just because it's hard to turn off a crush instantly. My intentions are good. I can't crush on him. He's a movie star. I'm just me. And this is Julie's night, after all. I need to focus on Julie. The last thing I should be doing is letting my thoughts go wild with wonder over what Trevor thinks. He had kissed me back, after all. If he'd thought I was ugly and boring, he'd have pushed me away and never kissed me.

And even though none of that matters because me trying to date a movie star would never actually work out, it brings me a lot of joy to know that he kissed me back. Maybe one day when I'm eighty years old, sitting around and talking to my grandchildren, I'll tell them of the time a famous movie star kissed me. And they'll want to know who, and we'll Google his name—and he'll be old by then but his movies will remain forever. *Oakbrook Lake* will still be around, probably on some streaming TV service, and I'll be able to point to the parts of the film that have my body and Andrea's CGI face, and I'll say, "That's your grandma!"

I'm lost in thoughts of this imaginary future when Trevor leans over so close I can smell his cologne, which pulls me right back to the present. "Does every diner in Texas make such good food, or is it just this one?"

I chuckle. "I think this one is special. No one makes food this good."

"I'm going to miss it when I go back home. The food, and the service. Everyone is so friendly here." He pats his stomach, which from my point of view looks like it's still flat and perfect. "My trainer would kill me if he saw me eating this."

"Is your trainer here in Sterling?" I ask. For all I know, personal trainers travel with their famous clients to keep them in shape on the road.

He grins an evil but delightfully sexy grin. "Nope."

"Then what he doesn't know won't hurt him."

"Amen to that." Trevor lifts his glass in a toast, tapping it to mine.

Overhead, the music gets a little louder as people are finishing their meals and venturing to an empty part of the patio to dance. In the middle of the dancers are the happy couple, Julie and Max, who both look like they're absolutely glowing. I guess being in love brightens your spirit better than any lighting or makeup ever could.

I watch as Max spins Julie around the makeshift dancefloor, his adoring gaze never leaving his soon-to-be-wife. My heart warms and floods over with happiness for my best friend and her fiancé. Julie deserves this so much, especially after what her ex put her through. She's an amazing person inside and out, and seeing her so happy in love gives me so much joy.

"Would you like to dance?" Trevor asks. A few more couples have joined Julie and Max out on the patio, but the idea hadn't even crossed my mind.

"What? No way. I don't dance."

Trevor quirks an eyebrow.

"What?" I say, glancing away from his eyes which seem to pierce into my soul.

"You do too dance."

"No, I don't."

He leans toward me, his mouth just inches from my ear. "Then who was I dancing with in the ballroom of Sterling's banquet hall?"

The memories of that day—that kiss—flood back into me like a tidal wave of warmth. I swallow.

"Okay, well I guess that was dancing, but it was for the movie. It was acting."

He reaches over and brushes a strand of hair from my face, his fingers leaving a searing hot trail across my skin. "Annie, will you follow me to the patio dance-floor and *act* with me?"

I roll my eyes in an effort to hold back my smile. My heart thunders beneath my chest. "Fine," I say, taking the cloth napkin from my lap and laying it on the table.

He stands and holds out his hand to me. I take it, because it would be awkward not to, and I follow him out to the empty patio space, surrounded by a few other couples, while a slow Garth Brooks song plays.

My hands know right where to go. Trevor and I have danced before, and it was somehow less nerve-wracking that first day when we were surrounded by extras and actors and the film crew, those big warm lights overhead shining down on us. It was different. I was a nervous body-double with no idea what I was doing.

Now, I'm still nervous, I still have no idea what I'm doing, and I'm desperately trying to fall *out* of love with this man, not into it.

I take a deep breath and focus on my footwork. Trevor leads us in a slow dance, his feet steady and confident while mine are still trying to figure out what to do. I can feel his eyes on me, but I look anywhere but into his gaze. I look at his shoulder, at the buttons on his shirt, the little row of stitching that goes across his collar.

We dance through three songs, and while I'd hoped to get this over with quickly, now that we're together, moving in sync to the music, I don't really want to go back to my chair. Right now I feel like that meme of the cartoon guy sitting at a table surrounded by flames and saying, "this is fine."

This is fine, I tell myself.

Dancing with Trevor is totally fine. Nothing to see here.

But when we pass by Julie and Max on the dance floor, I look over and my eyes meet hers, and instead of doing something to extinguish these metaphorical flames all around me, she winks. *Some best friend she is*, I think with a sarcastic grin as I wink back at her.

Before I know it, the evening is over, and I'm saying goodbye to all the guests and thanking them for helping me throw this last-minute surprise engagement party. When I finish talking with Clare, I look around to find Trevor helping the staff clean up plates. I watch him for a moment, totally mesmerized that a man of his wealth and fame would hang around and help the staff do a boring, dirty job.

Once everyone is gone, and the party is cleaned up, Trevor drives me back home. Our conversation is light and fun, but not very flirty. I get nervous as he pulls into Julie's driveway. The butterflies in my stomach dance around as I wonder if he's going to kiss me goodbye.

"Thanks for inviting me," he says, giving me a

genuine smile. "I had a lot of fun. And everyone was really cool. No one treated me like a celebrity, which was nice."

"I'm glad," I say.

"It felt good just being a regular guy." His smile softens. "Thanks again."

"You are quite welcome," I say. Then I get out of his car.

He doesn't try to kiss me, which is exactly how he should act. I mean, I told him this wasn't a date. I told him I didn't like him. He's not supposed to kiss me.

Yet I still get a twinge of disappointment. My heart really needs to get its feelings under control.

The next few days are so fascinating to watch. My normally chill best friend is so happy with being engaged that all she does is float around the house now. She's always smiling, and baking cookies, and laughing. Max spends a lot of time over here too, but he's busy working during the day, so it'll be just Julie and me most of the time. She doesn't do any writing this week, saying she's too excited to sit at her desk and focus on writing for the time being.

I'm so thrilled for her, and just seeing her happy

makes me happy, too. I can almost forget about my short-lived gig working as an extra on a film set and that means I can almost forget about my huge crush on Trevor Owens. If I were still a little teenager, I'd probably be obsessing over him and writing his name on my binder and daydreaming about our future together. But I'm an adult now, so I do no such thing.

I even mute the name Trevor Owens on my Twitter feed so that I don't accidentally stumble across any articles about him. I know he's still in town since the film crew is still here, but soon they'll wrap up filming and he'll go back to Hollywood and I'll be able to breathe easier again by fully putting him—and my silly crush—into the rearview mirror of my mind.

Julie and I spend our days hanging out and enjoying being best friends with nothing to do for a few days. I'm still sending out job applications to every new opening because it is important to get a job, and I can't lose sight of that. As much as I'd love to stay here with my best friend forever, I can't. She'll get married soon and be living with Max. I need to get a job, and my own place and go back to being a responsible adult.

Julie and I are looking up wedding venues on her computer when I hear my phone ding with a new email. I light up when I see who it's from.

"It's the retirement home!" I say, eagerly opening the email.

Grace Elder Care is a nearby elderly living facility that is brand new and extremely nice. The residents basically live in luxury in the gorgeous, sprawling building that has two on-site restaurants, a golf course, a fitness center, a movie theater, and more. They're hiring for a full time nurse to work the day shift, and I had applied knowing it would be my dream job, but doubting I would get it.

"They want me to do a phone interview today!" I tell Julie.

"Yay!" she says, clapping her hands together. "This is your dream job and it's just a few miles away."

"I really hope I get it," I say, as I hit the reply button on my phone and type out a quick reply, letting them know I'm available at any time for a phone interview. A few minutes later, we've scheduled an interview call for two hours from now.

And two days after that, I get offered the job.

CHAPTER 18

Trevor

It's the last day of filming the movie *Oakbrook Lake*, and everything feels bittersweet. Most of the crew is ready to go back home or start working on their next project. Sterling, Texas was just a quick stop on the long road of a career in film for everyone else. But for me, it feels like a destination. It's the place I met the woman of my dreams. It's also the place where I lost her.

I've had dinner from Roger's Diner delivered to my hotel every day for the last few weeks because the food is amazing, but I don't have the energy to drive there myself. It's not even that I'm worried about fans noticing me. It's just that I don't want to see the place we danced and remember how much fun I'd had with

Annie that night before she told me she no longer liked me.

I made the mistake of confiding in my little brother last week. I'd stayed up late video chatting with him in my hotel room, telling him all about Annie and how I like her—I probably even love her —but she doesn't like me. In true younger brother fashion, he heckled me and poked fun of me and make jokes. But then he said that once filming wraps up and I leave this small Texas town, I'll never have to think about her again. He called her a blip in my life, something so short on the whole scale of life things that I won't even remember her in a year or two.

My brother is getting a Master's degree in physics and is smart about a lot of things, but I'm pretty sure he's wrong about this one. I won't forget about Annie. In fact, I think I'll spend the rest of my life regretting it if I don't take one more chance.

I spend an hour in hair and makeup today, doing three wardrobe changes for all three photoshoots I have to do with Andrea Block. We go on location, to the lake, the ballroom, and then to a small park beside the lake and take hundreds of photos together. They'll be used for promotion, movie trailers, the DVD cover, and stuff like that. It's so ironic how I can sit here with

Andrea Block in my arms, gazing into her eyes the way the photographer tells me to and still feel nothing.

This romance with Andrea is just acting. It's all fake, meant to draw viewers into a fictional romance on the screen. And I think we've done a good job of it. Andrea's arm stays out of each photo we take so the cast is hidden, and she looks up at me just as adoringly as I look at her. But my mind is a blank. My thoughts are of nothing romantic at all while I sit here, the camera flashing multiple times until we're asked to pose a slightly different way for the next set of pictures.

Yet when I'm around Annie, my thoughts are racing. They're filled with emotions and love and anxiety. But it's a good anxiety around Annie. It's a thrill and a rush and the hope of something that will last forever.

Somehow, I make it through the whole morning of promotional photoshoots, and then four hours of interviews with Andrea beside me. When it's all over and we're officially done with *Oakbrook Lake*, I walk outside of the Sterling Banquet Hall and stand on the balcony that overlooks the lake. It's a beautiful day outside, with perfect weather that's not too hot or too cold. The lake is calm, and the sky is a sunny and bright blue.

Annie had told me that we'd never work out

because I'm a movie star and she's a nurse. Because I live in California and she lives in Texas. Well, that's not totally true, though. She's also told me that she had lost her job and was living with her best friend. So in a way, she's jobless and has no permanent address right now. Why can't her address be in Los Angeles? Why can't she find a job doing what she loves but in another town? It makes sense to me.

Now I just need to find her and do what I should have done weeks ago.

Confess my love.

I went back to my hotel, showered, picked out an outfit of dark jeans and a black Henley shirt, and sent a photo of myself to my brother's girlfriend, Lucy, for approval. I normally wouldn't need the confidence boost of having someone tell me if I'm wearing the right thing. But this isn't a normal situation. I'm about to do something I've never done before. I want to go into this having done everything right—my clothes, my words, my timing. Luckily, Lucy said I looked great, and my brother, after teasing me a bit, agreed.

Now I'm in my rental car and driving across town, trying to remember the exact directions toward

Annie's friend's house. It's also lakefront property like my hotel, but it's on the far east side of the lake. Lake Sterling is so massive that you can stand on the waterfront and not be able to see across the whole thing.

My memory serves me well, and soon I see the little white house in the distance. Only Annie's car is in the driveway, which makes this a little easier. I'm not sure my love-confessing would be as genuine as possible if her friend were there to watch me make a fool of myself.

I park, nervously pocket the car keys and walk up to the front porch. I'm not sure why I'm so nervous. I don't even mind red carpet events anymore, not after a few years of practice. But talking to this woman? That makes my knees weak and my heart nervous. Because what if she says no? I brush the negative thoughts aside and refuse to let them cloud my happiness. I love Annie, and I can feel the connection between us. I think she can feel it, too.

I knock on the door. Moments pass before I hear any sound. Then, finally, I hear the *click* of the door unlocking. And then there she is.

Annie's dark hair is twisted into a messy bun on top of her head, secured with a pink velvety scrunchie. She's wearing pink sweatpants with little red hearts all over them and a black tank top. I just want to curl up on the couch with her all day, snuggling her close to me.

"Hey..." she says, eyeing me with a hint of skepticism as she pushes open the screen door.

"I'm sorry I showed up unannounced." I smile, hoping I'm not catching her at a bad time. "I don't have a way to contact you, so I thought I'd just..." I shrug. "Show up."

"It's fine," she says, stepping out onto the porch. I try not to take it as a bad sign that she came out here with me instead of inviting me inside. "What's up?"

There's still a reservation about her, a guarded wall she's put in place between us and I don't know why. But it trips me up, making me question if this is the right move to make. But I know deep down that if I don't confess my feelings for her right now, I'll end up regretting it forever.

"Annie," I say, reaching for her hand. To my delight, she reaches out to take it. "I make a living being fake," I say, hoping she can see in my eyes that I mean every word of what I'm about to say. "But I want to be real with you. I want to be everything with you."

CHAPTER 19

Annie

Trevor squeezes my hand and warmth floods into my fingers, rising straight up my arm. I barely hear the words he says because I'm not quite sure why he's saying them. Why did he show up here to announce all this stuff about wanting to be real? He's a famous movie star. I'm just a random woman in Texas. I thought we've already established that. We've already made it clear that there's no reason to continue being friends.

I look at his hand which is wrapped around mine. His skin is tan and warm. His fingernails are perfectly trimmed, probably by a professional in the hair and makeup trailer. Veins run across the top of his hand and then up his forearm. I notice all of this about him in just a few seconds. Then I let my hand slip from his grasp and fall to my side.

"I don't understand," I say, looking up at him. "What is this?"

His expression falters. "I'm trying to tell you that I'm in love with you."

My eyes widen.

Behind him, the sun shines brightly in the mid-morning spring air. Julie's flowerbeds are brightly colored, filling the porch with a beautiful floral scent. Somewhere off in the distance a bird sings. I notice every single inch of our surroundings because it's easier to look around at the earth instead of right in front of me.

"You're in love with me?" I ask, half expecting him to burst out laughing, telling me it's all a joke. Maybe a cameraman will pop out from behind his car and I'll be on a cruel reality TV show where famous people trick dumb commoners into thinking they'd ever have a chance with them.

But none of that happens. There's not even the slightest hint of a smile on Trevor's face. His lips, those perfectly soft and amazing lips, rest in a flat line on his impossibly gorgeous face. His eyes are focused on mine, his forehead smooth and serene. The lines of his face tell me this isn't a joke.

His breath hitches. "Yes, Annie. I know what it sounds like. And I know who I am, and who you are, and I don't care about any of the reasons that make it seem like we shouldn't be together. The only thing I care about is my feelings for you. My love for you."

My heart pounds against my ribcage. I have medical training and years of knowledge and I know this is just a silly bought of heart palpitations and not a heart attack, but gosh it kind of feels like one.

"I love you, Annie. I love you and I want you to move to LA with me because I can't imagine my life without you."

I can't believe I'm hearing these words. Not just from Trevor Owens, the movie star, but from Trevor, the man. A man loves me. A man who I think I love back. I've just been too scared to think it and way too scared to say it out loud. It felt silly, childish, to love a movie star.

He takes a step closer, bringing the scent of his cologne with him. I breathe it in, my eyes fluttering closed as he reaches up to touch my face. His thumb slides over my cheek. "Please tell me you feel the same way," he breathes.

I open my eyes. Peering up at him, all the reasons my brain can think of to run away are starting to fade from existence. It's hard to think clearly. I just want to fall into his arms and kiss him and never stop, but I'm not some lovesick little girl like I might have been years ago. I'm all grown up now, fully aware of how hard love can be. I'm aware of all the obstacles that stand in our way, namely his extremely famous career. Do I want to risk loving a man only to have it fall apart because of his fame?

It's only moments, but fear and love and happiness and anxiety take over me all at once.

"Annie?" Trevor says. "Should I leave? Are you okay?"

"No," I say quickly, then I smile when he looks worried. "I mean, no, don't leave. Yes, I'm okay. I'm just... stunned, I guess."

He runs his hand through his hair and takes a step back. "I'm sorry. I shouldn't have just showed up here and declared my love for you. I didn't mean to upset you."

"I'm not upset," I say, shaking my head. Then I grin. "This is the coolest thing that's ever happened to me."

This makes his worried expression perk into a smile. "Oh yeah?"

I nod. "Trevor... I do feel the same way. I..." Oh gosh, why can't I say I love him back? Why can't I just *say it?* I look into his hopeful eyes and a rush of emotion overtakes me. I lean up on my toes and grab his face and kiss him. It's a quick kiss, hard and full of emotion, but I don't give it time to develop into anything else before I pull away.

"Trevor, I got a job."

His eyebrow quirks up. "You did? Another acting job?"

I shake my head. "I was just offered my dream job here in Texas. Not far away, actually. It pays well and it's working with the elderly which has always been my dream career. I start next week."

"Right," he says, biting his bottom lip. "That's really great."

I nod eagerly, bursting at the seams with how excited I am for my new job. "It's really a perfect job. It's what I've wanted ever since I got my nursing degree, but I've never even had an interview for a job like this until now. So, I guess you can see why this is all so much for me to take in. I never expected you to have feelings for me. I thought I was being a total dork for developing feelings for you over the past few weeks because I didn't think you'd ever like me back."

His arms slide around my waist, holding me steady here on the porch. His lips are just inches from mine. "I definitely, definitely like you back," he says softly.

"You're all I can think about. I've never felt this way about anyone."

"But don't you see all the problems?" I feel like the world's biggest brat bringing this up right now. But if I don't stand up for myself, I'm in dire risk of getting hurt. "Trevor, you're wildly famous and handsome. What if I uproot my entire life and then you get bored of me? Or what if some beautiful, rich actress decides she wants you and you don't want me anymore?"

"Baby, that's never going to happen," he says, kissing my forehead. I feel his hands, strong and power- ful, slide up my back, gripping my waist as he holds me to him.

"I'm scared," I breathe against his chest.

"We don't have to rush anything." He peers down at me with a soft smile. "It's not like you have to pack up your life and rush off to LA with me right now. We can date. We can take our time. I can prove to you, however long it takes, that I'm in love with you and just you."

Again, the words stick in my throat and I can't seem to make myself say them back. Admitting I love Trevor will be opening myself up to getting hurt. I peer up at him, my hands resting on his chest, his arms still holding me close, for several moments.

"I couldn't live with myself if I'd gone back home

without telling you how I feel," Trevor says, letting his arms go. He takes a step back, which brings some much needed space between us and now my brain feels like it can function a little better now that I'm not wrapped up in how handsome he is. He takes my hand and squeezes it. "Why don't you take some time to think about it? You don't have to answer me now. I'll come back later if you want me to. We could have dinner or something."

I nod slowly, not because I want him to go, but because he's probably right. I need to shower and get dressed and clear my head and think about this.

"I feel like this is one of those moments in the movies where the guy tells the girl he loves her and the girl says she loves him and they hug and live happily ever after, and I've just screwed it all up."

He chuckles. "You haven't screwed up anything. This isn't *Oakbrook Lake*. This is real life. Real life can be messy. That's what makes it real."

His words comfort me.

"Come back in an hour?" I ask.

"Sure."

He leans forward and kisses me on the cheek.

As he walks toward his car, I call his name.

He turns around.

I smile. "I love you."

CHAPTER 20

Trevor

She loves me.

The wheels of my rental car may be on the ground but my head is on cloud nine. I drive back to the hotel with an amazing feeling of love radiating from me. I've never been this happy in my life. Nothing can bring me down.

I offered to leave Annie's house so she could take some time alone to think about things. I didn't want to leave, of course, but I had just dropped a huge emotional bomb on her lap and I didn't want her to feel pressured into anything. I want her to think it through and decide if she truly loves me the way I love her.

Back at my hotel, my things are mostly packed since I'm supposed to leave soon. The film crew has only paid for the hotel up until today, but I paid for the rest of the week myself. I'm just not ready to go home yet. My agent is in talks with getting my next movie contract done, but for now, I don't have anywhere to be. And I only want to be with Annie.

I grab a coffee from the hotel's restaurant and take it up to my room. With the rest of the film crew gone, the fans have faded away and no one thinks to look for me here since they must assume I've left, too. It's nice being able to walk freely, just like it had been that night at the engagement party. It makes me think of what my life would be like if I left acting for good.

I'll probably always retain a bit of fame, but over the years, I'd slip from people's minds and maybe they wouldn't recognize me anymore. Maybe I could live a normal, calm life. Maybe it could be here, with Annie.

My throat swells up with emotion. I *could* do that, sure. But I can't right now. I still need more money to take care of my mom and pay off her house and all of her other bills. Then, I need to save up enough money to buy a house for Annie and me and to figure out what I want to do after my acting career is over. I have a degree in electrical engineering, so maybe I could get a regular job. But not yet.

Annie and I could have a long distance relationship for a few years, just until I'm rich enough to give up my acting career. Could I do that? Could I be away from her?

I open up my laptop and send an email to my assistant, asking her to find me a rental property here in Sterling. She replies back almost instantly, just a string of question marks.

I'm looking for a vacation home, a place to stay when I'm not working, I reply. Then, even though my assistant is sworn to confidentiality about everything in my life, I add another sentence just to make sure: *Please keep this between us.*

A few minutes later, she sends me a selection of apartments, condos, and rental homes. None of them are exactly in Sterling, Texas because it's such a small town, but they're nearby. I look through them excitedly, so eager to have a place close to Annie where I can escape Hollywood life and take her on romantic dates and spend time getting to know each other.

The hour passes slowly, as time tends to do when you're looking forward to something, but soon it's been a full hour and I get ready to go back to her house. I close my laptop and tuck it away in its protective sleeve. My phone starts buzzing, which is a helpful reminder that I still don't have Annie's phone number.

It's my agent, probably calling to let me know he secured a new movie deal for me. I let it go to voicemail. Sure, a new deal will be great, but I'm already in such a great mood that I don't care about anything else right now.

My assistant calls me just moments later as I'm walking out my hotel room. This time I do answer, since she's looking for rental properties for me.

"What's the good news?" I say instead of hello.

"It's not good," she says. There's a weird tone in her voice that I've never heard before. "Trevor, have you been on social media?"

I stop in the doorway, wondering if whatever she's talking about is worth stopping and opening my laptop again. "No, why?"

"You're supposed to let me know if you're partying around, being wild and crazy," she says, sounding a little maternal right now. "That's the deal. You let me know if there's something that could tarnish your reputation so I can get ahead of it if it does."

"What on earth are you talking about?" I ask, walking back inside my hotel room.

She breathes a heavy sigh. "Why don't you check Twitter and then call me back and let me know how I'm supposed to handle this PR nightmare."

The call ends and I stand here feeling stupid. What could possibly be a PR nightmare? I open the Twitter app on my phone and am inundated with 8264 notifications. My mouth falls open in horror as I look at the trending post for #TrevorOwens.

It's a picture of Annie and me in my trailer on set for *Oakbrook Lake*. She's wearing a bathrobe, which implies she's naked underneath. She's also sitting in my lap. And we're both just inches away from kissing. That had been an amazing day, but now seeing a picture of that moment here on my phone, on Twitter of all places, the memories turn sour in my mind.

The media is blowing up with speculation of this "mystery woman" and what we were doing in my trailer. I'm America's Sweetheart, the chaste, good guy. Now tarnished with a salacious picture, which, if I look at it from the perspective of a stranger it looks pretty darn bad. It looks like we've just made love.

The absolute worst part of all is that it's not a paparazzi photo. No one likes the paparazzi, but when they take photos of you, they're the bad guy. They're the ones sneaking around trying to snap an image of you doing something you shouldn't, or looking unflattering while at a restaurant shoving pizza in your mouth. Even when paparazzi photos make the headlines, there's a level of sympathy that people have for the victims in the photo.

But this is different. This isn't some sneaky shot from a snake in the paparazzi. This picture only existed on one device—one phone—so it could only have come from one person. Annie.

And I bet she got a lot of money for it, too. Probably easily thirty thousand dollars. Maybe even fifty. That day had been one of the best days of my life, and yet it turns out it was all a scam. It all suddenly makes sense to me—why Annie had been hesitant an hour ago when I revealed my love for her. She doesn't love me back. She just wanted to get close to me so she could catch me in a vulnerable position and then profit from it. Maybe she's not even a nurse at all. Maybe she's an aspiring actress who thinks having a sexy affair with a movie star will help her own career.

My throat feels like I swallowed a baseball. My heart is cold, lifeless. And the rest of me is battling the feeling of anger and betrayal and heartbreak. I loved Annie. I loved her with every inch of me. The first woman I've truly loved. I think that makes it hurt even worse.

She sold out a photo of us to the media. She profited on an intimate private moment. I can't believe one of the most special moments of my life meant nothing to her. I can't believe I fell for it.

Mostly, I can't believe that my heart still wants to love her.

Annie

When Julie gets home from visiting her grandmother, I rush outside and fly off the porch, so eager to tell her that Trevor loves me that I almost knock her to the ground when I skid to a stop in front of her car door.

"Are you okay?" she says, grabbing my arms to give me a look over. But there's nothing broken or bleeding here. Just happiness. Just tons and tons of happiness.

"I'm better than okay," I say, bouncing on my toes. I put my hands to my mouth, barely able to keep from squealing in delight.

"What's going on?" Julie looks behind me at the porch, and around the front yard as if the answer to her question will be standing here, a big bright neon elephant dancing in a tutu.

"I don't even know how to say it." I can't stop

grinning. I don't even have all the answers yet—*where will I live? Do I take my dream job or move to LA?*—but none of that matters. I can just feel it deep down in my bones that Trevor and I are meant to be. And what's meant to be will always find a way.

"Oh my gosh, it's about a guy," Julie says as her best-friend-instincts must kick in while she looks at me. Her eyes widen. "Is it Trevor?"

I nod, my teeth digging into my bottom lip.

"Trevor the *movie star?*" she says as if she's still not sure any of this is happening. To be fair, I'm still kind of in shock about it all, too.

I nod again. "The very same one. Trevor Owens said he loves me."

Julie quickly slams her Jeep door closed then hooks her arm around mine and quickly walks toward the house. "You have to tell me every single detail. But we need coffee first."

Inside, she heads to her fancy coffee maker and gets to work brewing two cups of cappuccino. I'm not really sure I even need caffeine right now because I'm so in love I have more than enough energy flitting about inside my veins, but Julie adores coffee so I let her do her thing.

Also...I check my watch. "We have to make this

quick because I only have five minutes until he arrives."

"Then you better spill all the details fast," Julie says, pointing a finger at me. Her coffee machine spews and rattles as it brews the first cup of cappuccino.

I sit at the kitchen island, bouncing the balls of my feet on the barstool's foot rail. I tell her about Trevor's random appearance an hour ago, and how he poured out all his feelings and how I kind of screwed it up big time by being so hesitant. Julie is so focused on my story that she doesn't even take a sip from her coffee mug. She just rests on her elbows, hands cupping the mug while she watches me from across the kitchen island.

"I can't believe I hesitated," I say once I've finished summarizing the talk Trevor and I'd had just a short while ago on the front porch. "I mean, I'm really excited about this new job but... does a job matter more than true love?"

"Definitely not," she says with a snort of laughter. "Love matters more than anything. But he said you can take things slow, so maybe you can do both? You can work your dream job here while the two of you date."

"Long distance?" I say, curling my lip.

She waves away my fears with her hand. "Girl, he's

famous. He'll just hop on a jet and fly over to visit you every other day."

I roll my eyes. "That sounds very expensive."

She winks at me. "You're very worth it."

My teeth dig into my lip again. "I don't love the idea of being long distance, but I'm also smart enough not to rush off and move to another state just for a guy. And he's not just any guy, he's a celebrity. What if it doesn't work out?"

Julie puts a hand on my arm, instantly steadying my panicky thoughts. "Take it one day at a time, Annie. You have a man who just told you he loves you. That's a good thing. Stop trying to make it bad."

I nod, drawing in a deep breath. "You're right. Besides, he'll be here soon."

I grin and do a little shimmy dance on my barstool, then I check my watch again. "Actually he's a few minutes late."

I check out the front window just in case he's waiting in his car or something, but he's not here. Julie and I move to the living room where I've got a perfect view of the driveway and we finish our cappuccinos.

Half an hour passes, and then an hour. Julie turns one of our favorite baking competition shows on the television but it doesn't distract me enough to take away my worry. Maybe he's late because he got caught up doing movie star stuff. He's talked about his agent several times. Maybe some big famous producer wants him for a movie and he's on a Zoom call right now, working out the details. Maybe he'll show up later with an apology for being late and we'll kiss and everything will be perfect again.

Except I have the weirdest feeling in my chest. A painful knot of anxiety that sits just behind my sternum. It's a feeling like something isn't okay. I look over at Julie and she must sense my worry because she frowns.

"He's probably just running late," she says.

"I don't know. It feels worse than that."

"Has he texted you?"

I shake my head. "In all this time, we've never exchanged phone numbers."

"Well, where's your phone?" she asks, glancing around. "Maybe an emergency came up and he could have called the film people to get your number or something. You never know."

I rush to Julie's office where my phone is sitting on the wireless charger. I haven't checked it in a while because there's no point—I have a job offer, and my best friend is here with me, and Trevor doesn't have my number.

My anxiety ramps up to epic levels when I see my

phone screen. I didn't think it was possible to have so many notifications at once. Thirty-two missed phone calls, mostly from friends or family members I haven't talked to in years. Fifty texts. And so many social media notifications that my app just says "100+ notifications" on the screen.

Holy cow!

I rush back to the living room in a daze, so shocked that I'm not sure what to check first. Julie sits next to me on the couch, looking over my shoulder.

"Oh my," she says, eyes wide. "What happened?"

"I don't know!"

I swipe away the missed phone call notifications and then go to the texts, seeing my mom's name at the top. I click on her texts first.

Momma: Annie, what on earth is going on? A movie star???? Call me!

"How does she know already?" Julie asks.

I shrug. "I don't understand... I haven't even told anyone that I worked as a body-double on the film set!"

My confusion makes the world seem to slow down. In a panic, I click through various texts, but they all sound a lot like my mom's. Everyone is asking me what's going on with me and the movie star, but no one is telling me how they found out.

"Oh no," Julie says, looking up from her own phone. "I found out what's happening. It's all over Twitter."

"What?" I say, dropping my phone and reaching for hers. She pulls it back before I can grab it, her bottom lip curling nervously under her teeth. "I don't know how to tell you this..." She glances at the phone again. "And honestly... I don't know how this photo even got out."

"Tell me!" I snap.

She turns the phone screen toward me and my whole world falls apart.

CHAPTER 22

Annie

The next day is one of the hardest days I've ever endured. Trevor never showed up yesterday, and I guess I can't blame him. He would have discovered the same thing I did, only this affects his life way more than mine. The only explanation Julie and I could come up with is that he must think I purposely sold out the photo to the press, and that's why he never contacted me or came back over to see me. I guess I can't blame him.

I ended up deleting every single text on my phone, just wiping out everything with a tap of my finger instead of wasting my time entertaining everyone's prying questions about the photo of me and Trevor Owens that's circulating the internet. I called my mom and gave her the whole story. I assured her that no, I wasn't sleeping around with celebrities, and that yes, Trevor and I did have feelings for each other. Her biggest question was that if I didn't leak the photo, and Trevor didn't have the phone on his own phone, who leaked it?

She thought maybe I had been hacked, which was a horrifying thought. What if someone had secretly infiltrated my cell phone and was able to listen to everything I say or watch me through the phone camera without my knowledge? Julie and I go straight to Sterling's only cell phone store and talk to the manager about it. He checks out my phone and my account and says he doesn't think it's very likely, and then he has an idea that I can't believe I didn't think of first.

He asks if anyone besides me had access to my phone.

And then the truth hits me like a ton of bricks. I remember that day at the coffee shop when I ran into Jackie, the woman who also played an extra on the set of *Oakbrook Lake*. I'd stupidly shown her the photo of Trevor and me. And then I walked away, leaving my phone on the table. It was such a short time, but I guess it was long enough for her to have stolen the picture.

The guy at the cell phone store tells me to check

my texts to see if she texted it to herself, but I've already stupidly deleted all my texts so I can't be sure. He's such a nice guy though, that he helps me pull my phone records and check them against the contacts I have saved, but there are no messages sent to numbers I don't recognize. Then he tells me to check my email.

And sure enough, there it is. A blank email with no text or subject line, with just that one photo attached, sent to Jackie's email.

The horrible woman was so greedy and desperate to sell a photo to the paparazzi that she'd emailed the photo to herself in just a split second while I'd gone up to the counter to pay for my coffee.

My blood turns to ice as I stand here in Sterling's small cell phone store, my best friend beside me and the helpful manager watching me curiously.

"I can't believe she did that."

"You might have a lawsuit on your hands," he says.

"Thank you so much for your help," I tell him. "I think I need to go home so I can throw up and cry."

He frowns and looks to Julie. "Take care of her."

She nods and wraps an arm around me. "I will."

At home, I sit on the couch, wrapped in a fuzzy blanket. I feel like a zombie. I feel betrayed. Lost. Heartbroken. Angry.

Last night I'd spent some time looking through

social media even though I definitely shouldn't have. The Trever Owens fans are going crazy, demanding to know who this "harlot" "hussy" "tramp" is in the scandalous photo of him. The more professional media outlets are calling me the "Mystery Woman" who was caught posing with him. I can't believe I'm a Mystery Woman. It's so weird.

Some people claim it's probably a digitally manipulated photo because Trevor is too good of a man to be posing with a half-naked woman.

Um, hello, I was in a robe. I wasn't exactly half-naked like all these people say!

But the worst part is how this photo is single-handedly tarnishing Trevor's good guy image. He has a reputation as America's sweetheart. As the handsome actor who doesn't constantly hook up with women. Christian women adore him, and moms love him, and every film he's ever been in are always rated as something wholesome that the entire family can enjoy. In today's world of TV shows with lots of nudity and sex scenes, many people really value Trevor's clean image.

And now this accidentally racy photo of me with him is ruining that.

I feel awful.

I have no idea how to reach out to Trevor and let him know that I'm sorry and that I didn't purposely do this. I call the hotel the film crew were staying at, pretending to be a member of the crew who needs to talk to the casting director, and they tell me the last of the crew checked out yesterday, which dashes my hopes of going to the hotel and finding Trevor in person.

His social media accounts haven't been updated in a week. If Trevor had any desire to reach out to me, I think he would have done it by now. But he hasn't.

Two days pass and my hope that he might find a way to talk to me, to get my side of the story, diminishes. Things get even worse when I wake up the next morning and see a news headline under the #Trevor-Owens hashtag.

Trevor Owens Dropped From Future Acting Gigs with Oakbrook Lake Parent Company

Tears swell in my eyes as I read the article. Apparently, there's an ethics and character clause in his contract that states that he must conduct himself as an honorable person in order to star in the wholesome romance movies that made him famous. And that due to his inappropriate behavior with the Mystery Woman, they've decided to cancel his contract and no longer cast him in future movies.

I am heartbroken for him. My careless mistake of leaving my phone with Jackie has cost him extreme damage to his career. Social media is going crazy—half of his fans hate him and half of his fans still love him and instead hate me, the Mystery Woman.

And yet Trevor is still silent.

I have no idea what's going on in his mind. He probably hates me.

But I have to do something.

I wait until Julie goes to sleep because I worry she'll try to talk me out of this. What I'm about to do could be extremely stupid. Or maybe it's a great idea. But it's all I can think of to do, and I have to do something. Trevor doesn't doesn't deserve any of this bad press. He's an amazing guy and he deserves only the best.

I set my phone on the bookshelf in the office and I close and lock the door. Then I stand in front of my phone and press record.

CHAPTER 23

Trevor

When my mom discovered that my life had imploded basically overnight, she'd called me all concerned and worried as if I were still a little kid. She told me to quit acting and move back home with her. She's always on my side no matter what. She didn't ask if the supposed "Mystery Woman" was really a fling, or something else. She didn't ask me to talk about any of it. She just told me to come home and forget all about the mess of trying to be famous.

I almost did. I almost packed up my stuff and raced back to my hometown, but then I reminded myself of the reason I'm living in LA right now in the first place. I'm here because I'm good at acting, and I'm on a mission to earn enough money to make my mom financially set for life. Losing my contract with the one company that has given me most of my acting work is a huge setback, but it's not the end of the world. It can't be. I have to have faith that things will work out.

Even if things don't work out, even if my career is totally over, it doesn't even feel like the bombshell it should be. I guess because my heart is already broken from what Annie did to me. I'm not sure it can break anymore. If film companies want to fire me, then fine, so be it.

But Annie broke my heart and I'll never feel quite whole again. I loved her. I trusted her. She'd seemed so genuine, and real, and sweet. How can I ever trust anyone again?

I've stayed off the internet since the day I discovered that photo on social media. I flew home from that small Texas town and have been tucked away in my house ever since, ordering food delivered to my door so I don't have to go out or see anyone. My assistant calls me a few times a day to check in, and my agent has assured me that he won't let this ruin my career. I know I'll need to pull myself out of this pit of despair soon, but for now, I slump into my couch, click on the television, go to my favorite streaming app and watch a comedy I've seen a million times before.

My assistant texts me several times in a row. I tend to ignore all texts lately unless she sends a bunch at once, and I guess she's figured out that's the best way to get ahold of me these days. I reach over and pick up my phone, ignoring the multitude of other unread texts from friends, and clicking just on hers.

She sent a link.

I click on it and my heart throbs painfully when I see Annie's face on the screen. The title of her video is *I am the Mystery Woman*.

I sit up straight on the couch, holding my phone horizontally in my hand. I mentally debate if I should watch the video or not, but ultimately, seeing Annie's face on the screen breaks me to pieces. I want to see her, even if I'll hate what she has to say. But maybe, just maybe, this video will explain why she betrayed me. Obviously, she did it for the money. Rumor has it, the media paid over fifty grand for that one scandalous photo. But did she even care about me at all? Even a tiny bit? Does she at least feel bad about what she did?

I click play.

"My name is Annie Reyes," she says. Her voice is level and emotionless. "I am the mystery woman that everyone has been talking about in regard to a photo of me and Trevor Owens that was sold to the media."

She swallows and tucks her hair behind her ear. She's radiating nervousness, her lips trembling as she prepares to talk again. I lean closer to the screen.

"I have no way of contacting Trevor Owens because, contrary to what people online seem to think, I am not his lover, or secret fling, or whatever lies people are making up after seeing one simple photo. So I thought I'd make this video in the hopes that it would get back to him, and also to set the record straight. I'm tired of lies and terrible things being said about me, but I'm even more disturbed at how this has been taken completely out of context in an effort to ruin Trevor's career."

She breathes in deeply, then continues. "I was hired to play the body double for Andrea Block after she broke her arm and couldn't film for a few weeks. Because of my job, I was around Trevor every day for a while. One day, the costume crew lost my original clothes and so I was wearing *clothing* underneath a robe." She holds up her hand. "I wasn't naked. I wasn't even close to being naked. And Trevor and I were goofing off and I tripped and fell, which is why the photo you've all seen is blurry. It was taken quite literally as I was falling while trying to take a selfie."

She presses her lips together and shrugs. "That's it, guys. That's all. It was a silly photo that meant nothing. In my short time on film sets, actors goof off and play all the time. You can't judge someone's character off a split-second snapshot, and I'm disgusted that so many people have turned their backs on Trevor, an actor you all loved before this silly photo came out."

Damage control. That's what she's doing. She's trying to fix a problem she created. I pause the video and take a deep breath, clenching my jaw. I wonder why she's doing this now? Did my agent call her and ask her to settle what happened? Did someone from the press offer her more money to come forward? Probably.

I look back at my phone, wondering if I should even waste my time watching the rest of it. But then curiosity gets the best of me and I click play.

"As for how the photo got out, I'd like to set the record straight. That photo was on my phone, and only my phone. I've never sent it to anyone, and I never would. However, I recently figured out how it was stolen from me. A woman named Jackie snuck my phone when I wasn't around and emailed it to herself. I will attach a screenshot of the email at the end of this video. I had no idea she did this and I would never, ever, have approved it. In fact, I am stating this now because I think the casting crew should be aware of this woman, as she told me the day I met her that she purposely tries to find candid photos she can take and sell to the paparazzi, which is why she works as an extra in the first place. So if anyone is in charge of hiring movie extras, maybe look up this Jackie woman and stop hiring her, okay? The reputations of your actors are all at risk when she's on set and if you respect their privacy, you'll stop allowing this woman to work as an extra."

Annie is quiet for a moment, then she looks down for a bit before looking back at the camera. "I guess that's all I have to say."

The video ends and I sit here staring at my phone screen for a long time.

Well... this changes everything.

CHAPTER 24
Annie

Two Weeks Later

"Good morning, Mrs. Gomez," I say as I enter the elderly woman's room at Grace Elder Care. As a healthcare provider, I shouldn't have "favorites," but I secretly do. Mrs. Gomez is a firecracker of a woman, despite her thin frame and short stature. I like her because she's hilariously sarcastic and witty in a way that reminds me of the characters in my favorite irreverent TV shows. But she also cares a lot about people. She'd noticed right away that I was nursing a broken heart myself in addition to caring for my new patients when I started working here.

She wouldn't let it go until I decided to briefly

give her a description of what caused my broken heart. I told her he worked too far away and a big misunderstanding happened that ruined everything between us. She seems to think I'm being overly dramatic and should go seek him out to fix things between us. But that's only because I didn't give her all the details.

"Annie-banan-ie," she says, smiling up at me from her recliner. Her favorite pastime is diamond painting and crocheting, and today she has a half-finished diamond painting on the table next to her and a half-finished crocheted doll in her lap. The woman loves to multi-task. "How are you today?"

"I'm the nurse, I'm supposed to ask you that," I say playfully as I walk over and wrap the cuff around her upper arm so I can take her daily blood pressure reading.

"Oh, I am perfect," she says with a wave of her hand. "As always. Just watching these hunks on TV."

She nods up to the flat-screen television on her wall. She's always watching either reality TV shows, cooking shows, or those entertainment/TMZ type shows about celebrities. The woman may be elderly, but she keeps up with pop culture, that's for sure.

I chuckle and remove the arm cuff, then take her temperature and mark it in my company iPad, which keeps track of all my residents' vital signs and health records.

One thing I love about working at an elderly care center is that I get to bond with my patients. Things move slower here. It's not the hustle and panic of working in a busy urgent care, which I never really liked at my old job. Sure, things can get rushed here if a resident has a medical emergency, bust most days are slower and I can spend time with everyone, giving them company, friendship, and care.

"What on earth is this?" I ask as I examine Mrs. Gomez's unfinished diamond painting. It's a cartoonish picture of a giant pot leaf, which doesn't exactly seem like something she'd be into. The woman wears pastel colors and has crocheted doilies everywhere.

She chuckles. "Well, my grandson gave me that big gift card to buy more diamond paintings so I thought I'd make him one to show my gratitude. He can hang it in his dorm room," she says with an evil grin as if she's picturing a teenage boy hanging up his grandma's sparkly artwork in his dorm.

"You know that's a pot leaf, right?" I say. "It's weed? Like the drug?"

She rolls her eyes at me. "Oh, Annie, you're so silly. I wasn't born yesterday. Of course I know it's pot! But what can I say? My grandson thinks it's cool. He wants to move somewhere that weed is legal and I told him he'll only be able to afford that if he works hard in college and gets a good degree and a good job."

She chuckles to herself then looks back at the television. "Oh my, that's one handsome son of a gun right there."

I don't think twice about it when I look over to see what she's talking about, but instantly I regret it. A stock photo of Trevor Owens is on the screen. Then it shows footage of him walking on a red carpet, then goes back to another stock photo. The host of the celebrity news TV show is talking about him. I should look away. In fact, I should leave.

Mr. Albany lives next door and he only ever watches westerns on his TV. I should go check on him.

But my stupid heart takes over all bodily functions and keeps me rooted to the floor, my eyes watching the television. It's a short segment on the actor, one that's quickly replaced but another segment about a more famous actress and her contentious divorce from a billionaire tech mogul. In the few minutes Trevor is on screen though, I learn that he's just been signed on to star as superhero Max Knight in the City of Legends movie trilogy. It's a sharp contrast for him to go from playing sweet romance leads to an action superhero, but it'll do wonders for his career. Looks like he'll bounce back just fine after being fired from his former company because of that scandalous photo of us.

My throat feels like something is stuck in it. I'm happy that his career is doing better, but Trevor as a new superhero? That means his face will be all over the place. On kid's meal toys and T-shirts and school supplies. And internet memes and posters plastered all over the movie theater. How will I ever escape the constant reminder of the man I loved and lost?

It was so dumb of me to think that I could make that video online and that it would magically bring Trevor back to me. I'd hoped that by telling the truth, he'd learn what happened and forgive me for it. I was a nervous, anxious wreck for a week straight after I'd posted that video online. The possibility that he'd call or email or reach out to me felt so likely. Maybe even his manager would reach out. Or his assistant. Someone. Anyone.

Plenty of other people reached out to me. My video got two million views the last time I checked, and thousands of comments. #MysteryWoman was trending for a few days after the video went viral. As most internet trends do, it was popular for a couple days and then it faded away, replaced by the next dozen viral videos. Which is good, because I think it made a big enough splash that Trevor would have seen it, but not so big to ruin my life or anything. Besides Julie's friends in Sterling, no one has talked to me about it.

But I didn't make the video for the world. I made it for one person. And it's been radio silence from Trevor Owens for two weeks now.

I had to let it go. To let him go. I had to accept my fate and move on with my life, otherwise my heartbreak would ruin me. While Mrs. Gomez noticed it right away the day I met her, no one else seems to care, and I prefer it that way. I'm moving on. I'm working my dream job and living as a single woman who just moved out of Julie's house and into her own apartment. Everything else in my life will be okay, and my broken heart will just have to deal with it.

"Well, what do you think?" Mrs. Gomez says.

"Huh?" I look over, realizing she's been talking this whole time but I was too lost in thought, staring at the TV screen to pay attention to what she said. "Sorry, I —got distracted."

"I said what's your favorite color? I'm going to crochet you a little present."

"Oh, um..." I consider it. I usually say purple, or pink, but as I look at the wide array of yarn colors in her bag of crochet supplies, a teal color pops out at me. "This one."

"Perfect," she says, setting aside the piece she was working on and reaching for the teal yarn.

The radio on my hip beeps and my manager Ashleigh's voice says, "Annie, come to the front."

My eyes widen. Usually when my manager calls me on the radio she's asking for assistance in another room. But *come to the front* sounds bad.

"Am I in trouble?" I wonder out loud.

Mrs. Gomez presses her lips into a flat line. "You better not be. They'll have to deal with me if so." She stands up. "Let's go see what they want."

"No, it's fine," I say, not wanting to be humiliated in front of one of my patients if I am in trouble for something. "You can stay."

She shakes her head. She is a small woman, but a fierce one. "I'm going, now come on."

She makes her way to the door and down the hallway, so I follow, quickly getting in front of her so it doesn't look like I'm purposely asking a resident to fight my battles for me. We make our way down the main hallway toward the front desk.

I've loved every moment of my new job and I really hope I'm not in trouble. But when I approach the front desk, Ashleigh gives me the weirdest look. Immediately, I know I'm not in any kind of trouble with my job, but that something weird is happening. Her eyes widen and she rushes up to me.

"Oh my gosh," she whispers.

"What?" I whisper back.

"Talk louder," Mrs. Gomez says from beside me. "My old ears can't hear whispers."

"You have a visitor," Ashleigh says, nodding her head toward the waiting room next door.

"Is that so?" Mrs. Gomez says, walking toward the waiting room.

I quirk an eyebrow at my boss. Who would come visit me? Julie is busy working on her next novel and my parents live several states away. I'm so confused, but mostly, I'm glad to find out that I'm not in trouble at my new job.

"Girl, I wouldn't keep him waiting," Ashleigh says, grinning at me as she wiggles her eyebrows. She pushes me toward the door that leads to the waiting room and whispers, "You are a very lucky woman."

Time seems to slow down as I walk the short distance to the waiting room. It's a large room, filled with couches and nice chairs for family members to wait when they come to visit their relatives but can't go in their room for whatever reason. Sometimes the residents are showering or getting medical care and can't have visitors just yet.

I think somewhere deep down, *very, very, deep down*, my subconscious knows. But my brain is scattered with anxious thoughts and worries and the fear that I'll get my hopes up for nothing as I step through the door. The first thing I see is Mrs. Gomez.

"Are my eyes deceiving me or is that gentlemen the same one on the TV?" she says to me before looking back at the man standing sheepishly near a large houseplant.

"Oh my gosh," I say as my eyes meet Trevor's. He's wearing dark jeans and a white T-shirt. He looks a thousand times more handsome in real life than on the TV screen.

I spent a week hoping this day would come. And then another week convincing myself it never would. But he's here.

"Wait, are you the guy on the TV?" Mrs. Gomez says, totally unaware of how I am internally freaking out right now.

Trevor smiles. "Yes, ma'am."

"And you're here to see my Annie?" she asks, suddenly in control of the conversation.

Trevor nods. "Yes, ma'am. I'd like to speak with her if that's okay."

Mrs. Gomez folds her arms across her chest. "Sure.

But anything you have to say to my Annie you can say in front of me."

I can't help but smirk. Trevor looks at me with a tiny bit of fear in his eyes.

"She's protective," I say.

He nods once. "Okay, well, here goes." He presses his hands together in front of his chest, then takes a deep breath. "I still love you."

My chest floods with a happiness I've never felt before. I spent days dreaming of those words, but I never thought I'd hear them again.

Beside me, Mrs. Gomez gasps. "Boy, you better choose your words carefully because if you break my Annie's heart, you will have hell to pay."

"Yes, ma'am," he says with a solemn nod. "I understand. And I won't, I promise."

She nods once, looking him up and down. Then she turns to me. "Looks like you two have some making up to do," she says with a wink. "I'll be in my room, waiting patiently to hear all the details when it's done."

With that, she turns on her heel and walks out of here. It would be a little bit funny having an eighty-year-old woman take charge of my life if I wasn't standing here in shock.

"I am terrified of her," Trevor says after she's left

the room.

I can't help but smile. "She's amazing."

We stand here, so close and yet so far away. The room is empty now but visitors could come in at any moment. It feels like everything I want to say is just too much to say at once. Luckily, Trevor talks first.

"I saw your video." He takes a step toward me. "My manager confirmed what you said. They found the woman who sold the photo and she's been fired and blacklisted from ever working in the industry again. She also admitted to what she'd done... stealing that photo from your phone without your consent."

"I'm glad," I say, nodding slightly. I hate standing here all stiff like a robot, but my heart is very fragile right now and I'm not sure what to do. Why is he here? If he just wanted to tell me he saw the video I made, he could have done that over email.

"So... elephant in the room," he says with the smallest smile on his lips as he takes another step closer to me. We're now just a few inches apart. "I said I still love you and you didn't say anything back..."

"I don't know what to say," I admit. "I don't want my heart broken again."

"I'm so sorry I left without saying anything." The pained expression on his face is completely genuine. His brows knit together. "I was hurt, and also really confused—I didn't think you'd betray me like that, and I should have known it for a fact. I shouldn't have just left, without talking to you first. I'm so sorry."

"It's okay." He looks so pained and I feel so bad about it. I want to take all his pain away as quickly as possible so I keep talking. "Seriously, Trevor, it's fine. You're a famous movie star and you had to get back home, and it only makes sense that you'd leave. You didn't owe me anything."

He shakes his head. "No, I did. I love you, Annie. I love you with all my heart. I should have come to you first to learn the truth. And if you take me back, I promise I'll never leave again."

I swallow. He wants me back?

"What about your superhero movie deal?"

"That deal is the best thing to happen to me," he says. "Well, besides meeting you. The studio plans to shoot all three movies back to back over six months. And this isn't just some made-for-TV movie, this is the big leagues." His eyes sparkle with energy. "Annie, they're paying me so much money for this role. Like... insane money." He snorts and shakes his head. "It'll be six months of filming, and we'd have to be long distance, but six months isn't too long, and then I can retire from acting for good. And I can move here and start a life with you."

He reaches out a hand and lets his fingers slide down my forearm, stopping at my fingertips. I curl my hand to keep his laced with mine. "That is, of course, if you want me to," he says, inching just a little bit closer to me. I can smell his cologne, that delicious, fresh outdoor scent that feels like it's beckoning to me.

I gaze up into his eyes and feel the sincerity, the *love*, that pours out of him. I've never felt so sure about anything in my life.

"I want that very much." I lean up on my toes and kiss him.

His arms wrap around me and hold me tightly. I know in this moment that I'll never tire of being around this man. He is my perfect match in every way.

His lips press to mine, a familiar, yet delicate feeling that floods every cell of my body with love. He kisses me again, and again, and again. And then I'm giggling while wrapped in his arms, my heart feeling lighter than a feather.

"Come on," he says, taking my hand. "Let's go tell that terrifying woman the good news."

About the Author

Amy Sparling is the bestselling author of books for teens and the teens at heart. She lives on the coast of Texas with her family, her spoiled rotten pets, and a huge pile of books. She graduated with a degree in English and has worked at a bookstore, coffee shop, and a fashion boutique. Her fashion skills aren't the best, but luckily she turned her love of coffee and books into a writing career that means she can work in her pajamas. Her favorite things are coffee, book boyfriends, and Netflix binges.

She's always loved reading books from R. L. Stine's Fear Street series, to The Baby Sitter's Club series by Ann, Martin, and of course, Twilight. She started writing her own books in 2010 and now publishes several books a year. Amy loves getting messages from her readers and responds to every single one! Connect with her on one of the links below.

www.AmySparling.com

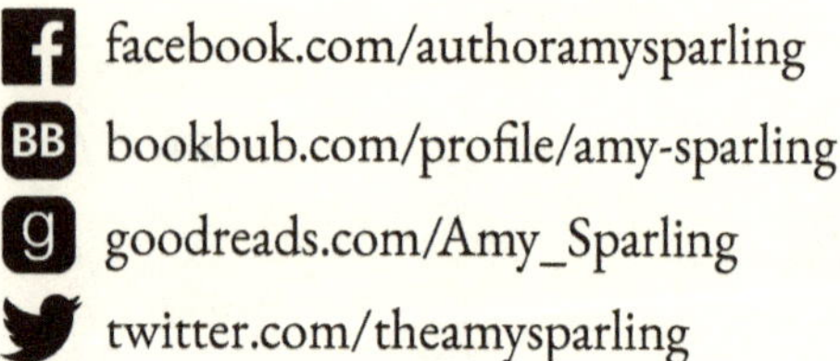

facebook.com/authoramysparling

bookbub.com/profile/amy-sparling

goodreads.com/Amy_Sparling

twitter.com/theamysparling

www.ingramcontent.com/pod-product-compliance
Lightning Source LLC
Chambersburg PA
CBHW021435150726
47989CB00001B/261